STILETTO
NIGHTS

STILETTO NIGHTS

SHYY

authorHOUSE®

AuthorHouse™
1663 Liberty Drive
Bloomington, IN 47403
www.authorhouse.com
Phone: 1-800-839-8640

This is a work of fiction. Names, characters, place, and incidents either are the product of the author's imagination or are used fictitiously. Any resemblance to actual persons, living or dead, events, or locales is entirely coincidental.

Published by AuthorHouse   06/21/2013

ISBN: 978-1-4817-6294-6 (sc)
ISBN: 978-1-4817-6293-9 (e)

Library of Congress Control Number: 2013910721

Any people depicted in stock imagery provided by Thinkstock are models, and such images are being used for illustrative purposes only.
Certain stock imagery © Thinkstock.

This book is printed on acid-free paper.

Because of the dynamic nature of the Internet, any web addresses or links contained in this book may have changed since publication and may no longer be valid. The views expressed in this work are solely those of the author and do not necessarily reflect the views of the publisher, and the publisher hereby disclaims any responsibility for them.

TABLE OF CONTENTS

The Affair

One Night Stand

Quiet of Night

Keeping Secrets

Temporary Insanity

To Love Me

Dedicated to those who have loved . . .

. . . but who have never been satisfied.

FOREWORD

Many of us are afraid to let ourselves go and to be moved by strong emotions. We fear what others might think or what we might see looking back at us when we look into the mirror of fantasy. These short stories were written for those of us who want to release our inhibitions. Go on and take a look. Remember—don't be shy.

ACKNOWLEDGMENTS

Thank you to my mother, "Queen Bee" who always believed that I had a talent to write. I miss you.

To my father who has taught me the power of finding forgiveness.

Hugs and Kisses to my daughters whom I hope know how much I love and adore them.

To my grandchildren, who will not read this until they are adults, you are my heart and soul.

Jose you are a good-hearted person. Thanks for always looking out for me.

To my five brothers who have always had my back. You have always made me proud.

To my girls who have rolled with me since elementary school—Pam R. (my cuz) Janice O. (my style Diva), Pam K. (my rock) and Sheila M. (Deceased—she kept me laughing). You all are the best. Thank you for all of your support and for being there for me.

To my family members who have gone on before me I know that you are on my shoulders.

To my family that is still here with me—there are no words to tell you how much you mean to me.

Renee M. my spiritual healer, you are beautiful. It is a blessing to have you in my life.

To Jo. We fight but that's what sisters do.

T-man thanks for the dance. I might forget the steps but not you.

Robert—You will always be my folks.

To my co-workers who have patted me on my back for more than thirty years, I miss you all.

To everyone who has touched my life and inspired me—I am eternally grateful.

And last but never least, to my husband "G." Without you I would have never known true love.

STILETTOS

Maybe I will wear my hair up
with just a single curl to grace my face
the cotton lingerie I normally wear
I will replace with satin and lace

my hands will massage my body with oils
with hints of fruit that will want to be tasted
lavishing myself with only the finest of things
when you are worth it money is never wasted

thoughts of candle light and champagne
a little slow dancing makes me smile
tonight I am going to be pampered
I can admit that it has been awhile

the reflection in the mirror
shows me that age has been thoughtful and kind
I plan on taking advantage
finally I am putting myself at the front of the line

I will slither into my sinfully red dress
I had forgotten how sexy it makes me feel
just like when I am putting on
or perhaps taking off my Stiletto heels.

STILETTO NIGHTS

Everyone has a down time at some point and time in their life. Times when they feel out of sorts and even out of touch with life. The problem with myself was that I had begun to feel out of touch with life so much that I had forgotten all of what it had to offer. And most importantly what I could still bring to it. For the past two and a half years I had spent my time crying and living in misery. My marriage was in shambles, my children were grown and had moved on and my mother had died suddenly. Like I have always said, "Shit happens and it's not always in your pants." My mother had always believed that I was going to become a journalist because of my strong passion for writing. I loved to write poetry and short stories but between the tragedies and the loneliness I had begun to shut down. Nothing seemed to fit anymore. Those who I thought would be there for me were not unless there were dramas that they could gossip about. Though it was a painful process I learned the definition of true friendship and I realized how little I had. Or at least felt that I had. My spirit was gone and I kept trying to find a way to get it back but nothing could triumph over my sadness, my hurt and eventually my will to live. There were many days and nights I just sat alone crying. Sometimes too afraid to leave the bed because I did not know what I might do. Then one day while I was lying in that very bed I glanced over at the shoe bag that was hanging on the back of my door. There were twelve pairs of shoes and among them was this one pair of sexy red stilettos. I went over to the shoe bag and took them out. I held them in my hands just for a moment and examined them as if I had never seen them before. I walked over to my full-length mirror and placing them onto the floor I balanced myself while I put my feet into them. I swear it was as if I had become Cinderella. I turned around so that I could see the back of my legs in the mirror. They were hot, hot, hot! Now mind you, I was standing there in my fruit of the loom panties and a bra but the stilettos made me look and feel as if I was a model on a fashion runway. I started posing in front of the mirror as if there were a photographer in the room. Suddenly I stopped and moved closer to the mirror and I smiled at myself and then I kissed my reflection. I threw my hands into the air and shouted, "I am back!" Finally I was seeing what everyone had been trying to get me to realize. Yes I had been hurt but I was still alive and still beautiful and vibrant. Who would have thought that a pair of red stilettos

that's right I am going to go get it on!" He smiled back
at me as if to say, "All right now—you go girl!" I felt
good inside. I felt confidant and guilt free. I text my
friend to make sure that everything was still on for our
rendezvous and to my delight it was. After a few more
stops I returned home and prepared for the night.
After taking a long bubble bath I perfumed all of the
hot spots and then put on my stilettos. I stood in front
of the mirror and stepped into my thong. My body
was long and lean and even though I was well over
thirty I was still in good shape. There was only a small
sign of my giving birth to two children so I decided
that it was time to get back into the gym to firm a few
things up. But all in all I looked good if I had to say
so myself. I put on the Chemise teddy and rubbed my
hands across the softness of the fabric and turned my
backside slightly towards the mirror to give myself a
booty check. It was purr-fect! It was chilly outside so
I put on my ankle length black tailored coat and
buttoned it just enough to leave an opening so that
when I walked you could see just the right amount of
leg to tease any man. When I arrived at his condo he
came out and met me at my car. He opened the door
and extended his hand to help me out and my coat fell
open to reveal my bare thighs. His eyes widened and I
knew he wanted to jump up and down even before he

He smiled and said, "Umm that feels so soft and nice." He leaned forward to kiss me. The kiss was delicate and just lightly on my lips. I wiggled the coat from beneath me and pushed it to the floor. He slid the spaghetti straps down from my shoulders and pulled the Chemise down until my breasts were fully exposed. He leaned forward and kissed each one making sure that they both received equal attention. He placed his hands on my hips and pulled me further forward towards him. His eyes were locked into mine. He kissed me again this time parting my lips so that I could feel his tongue. It was passionate but not lingering. His eyes never left mine and without looking down he then spread my legs open. He pushed the table back and went to his knees. He kissed my inner thighs until he made his way to my opening. He inserted his tongue and my body jerked and my back arched. He moved his tongue in and out and I couldn't help but to lick my lips. I moaned at the pleasure he was bringing to me as he found my clit and fondled it with his tongue. Suddenly he placed his full mouth over my opening and like a vacuum he sucked and licked me until my body was in a full frenzy. I grabbed onto his head so that he would not stop. He could not stop the pleasure that he was bringing to me because it was too damn good. I threw my legs around his stilettos raised high in the air I came and I came and I came. We fell backwards onto the sofa both exhausted and satisfied. When I returned home that night I felt as though something had awakened inside of me. I was no longer going to feel sorry for myself and I realized that I had been choosing to be alone. My life had changed and I had to make a decision on how to live with those changes. And so I did. I was going to embrace each day and night to the fullest and accept all that life was offering to me one pair of stilettos at a time.

NO COMMITMENT

The sound of the water running in the shower woke me. I leaned over the side of the bed and glanced at the crystal clock that sat on the mahogany nightstand. I covered my head. Damien had spent the weekend with me but now he had to return to New York to his other life. I knew that I should not complain because I knew that he was married and had children. But I was falling in love with him. Just the mere thought of him made me moist in my private places. Secret places that only he was allowed to venture into. I closed my eyes and relived the first time that we had made love. That's the nice way of putting it. I had on a tight red spandex dress that zipped up the front with a very thin thong underneath and black and red stilettos. We were in his office finishing up the last conference reports for our boss when he asked if I wanted something cool to drink. I unzipped the front of my dress slightly until you could see the deep cleavage just above the nipples of my breasts. Watching his eyes I knew he had grown like Pinocchio. But it wasn't his nose it was his manhood. I licked my lips and backed away and sat on the edge of the adjustable computer chair. I looked at him and said, "It is a little warm in here. I could use something cold and wet." Damien swallowed and said, "I'll go and get us something. In fact are you hungry? I can order take out or we can go and get something to eat." I slid back in the chair and pulled down on the zipper of my dress so that he could see the firmness in the nipples of my breast. I smiled a wicked smile and said, "I got milk. So why go out to eat when your happy meal is right here?" I threw my right leg over the arm of the chair and waited for him to respond. At first he looked as if he had died and gone to Heaven but the Angel on his shoulder was tugging on his conscience. I needed to pull out all of the stops. I started the party without him and began stroking myself seductively and he watched liked it was football season and his team was winning the Super Bowl. The next thing I knew his halo was gone and the fire from the devil was between my legs. I could have never imagined the ride that this man was taking me on. We almost broke the chair so we made our way to the wall and he was behind me. The coolness of the concrete on my nipples aroused me even more. He had one of his hands entangled in my hair pulling it as though he was riding a stallion. The other was pressed against my forest and pressing me closer to his manhood as he moaned and grunted. I felt his breath against my neck and turned slightly wanting to taste

11

him back and asked him where and when. His e-mail came back telling me to look in my desk drawer. I opened the drawer and there was a small box. Inside of the box there was a key to the company storage room and a piece of paper that had 12 noon written on it. It was now eleven forty-five. I crossed my legs to hold back my anticipation. I began to wish that I had not dressed so conservatively and in so many layers. Then it came to me that it was raining outside. I quickly got up and grabbed my coat and my gym bag from my file cabinet and went to the ladies room. I undressed and put everything into the bag. I sprayed on my perfume and put on my trench coat and headed to the elevator. As I walked down the hallway my boss yelled after me. I stopped in my tracks and he came up behind me. "Stacey I need you to run an errand for me if you can. I see that you are on your way out and I need this package dropped off at the post office. I would send it through the mailroom but I need it to go out today. Would that be an inconvenience for you?"

I turned around and smiled at him and said, "No not at all Mr. Redman. I might need a few extra minutes getting back though."

He looked down at the gym bag. "I see you're planning to workout on your break. Tack on an extra thirty minutes for your lunch and then stop by the post office on your way back. I appreciate your doing this for me."

I told Mr. Redman the pleasure was all mine and that his extra thirty minutes would be very beneficial to my workout. I headed towards the elevator again and pushed the button-marked basement. When I got off of the elevator it was dark and dreary as I walked down the hallway. I went to the door marked storage room and unlocked it with the key. As soon as I opened it Damien grabbed me and pushed me against the file cabinet. His tongue entered into my mouth and I melted like butter. He pulled back and looked at me and asked, "What's up with the coat?" I unbuttoned the trench coat and his eyes were as wide as his smile. He took my breasts in his hands and licked and pulled each nipple. As he nibbled his appetizers his main course was getting hotter and hotter. I rapidly removed the coat. It fell to the floor and I leaned back against the filing cabinet. The cold metal on my buttocks sent a wave of electricity through me that made me touch myself. That made Damien savor me even more. His tongue found his way down to my belly button and then to my thighs. I couldn't stand much more so I pushed his head down south and urged him on. He found the spot and lifting my legs over his broad shoulders he had lunch. His tongue went so deep that I know his tonsils touched my secret place. I was trying to grab hold of something, anything so that I could enjoy the ride. I felt my head go back. I tried to arch my back so that he could go further. Then when I thought I could not take any more he began to suckle me. I wrapped my legs around his head and I did not care if he could breathe or if I could breathe. I felt myself coming and I begged him to stop. Then I begged him not to stop. He pulled away and stood up. He turned me around and I felt him enter me. I moved my buttocks against the silkiness of his skin. I was so moist that it made him penetrate further with ease. He moaned and called me baby and told me what he wanted to do. I imagined all that I was not living at that moment. I touched myself and he encouraged me to. Then the sound of the file cabinet banging against the floor was all I heard as I screamed, "Oh Damien, oh Damien!" We were both out of breath and barely able to stand. He looked at me and smiled and asked, "Are you okay?" I let out a seductive chuckle and asked him, "That's all you got?" He smacked me on my buttocks and looked at his watch. Lunchtime

I to know if I was giving up a good thing or a piece of SHIT. Sex had changed a whole hell of a lot since then. I would always hear that married men would not do certain things with their wives that they would do with their mistresses. So I decided that I would flip the script. I would find me a single man and do what my husband thought I would not do for him. And I do underline the word <u>thought</u>. Some of you may say that I was putting myself at his level. I would say that you are absolutely right but I didn't start the game. And I did change the rules a little. The key word here being a single man. I would never involve myself with a married man under any circumstances. Think about it this way, I could have stayed home and cried my eyes out but what would have changed? I could have gone to an attorney and filed for divorce but I was not certain if this was the end of the road for us. Yes he cheated but how do I know that it was not for a good reason if I didn't try it out for myself. I mean I wanted to be fair about this thing, didn't I? Our intimate life was satisfying but it didn't always have the butta bing butta boom that I heard folks talk about. I wanted to take a slow ride on a big horse if you know what I mean. Don't get me wrong, my husband had taken me around the world a few times but if it takes more than eighty days than you need a little more helium in your balloon. But I will be fair and admit that it could have been me. I never hung from the ceiling, or tied him up in chains or . . . well that was about it. But if he had requested those two things I would have obliged. Anyway I needed to be sure that I wasn't sexually inadequate didn't I? It was Tuesday night and my girls and I always went to Club Nine. They had the best ribs in town. We would eat until our stomachs could not hold anymore and then we would go upstairs to party. This Tuesday was different; I was scanning the room because I was on a mission. I told my girlfriends Shayna and Jakee that I was ready to go because the place seemed a little dead. Then in he walked, BDT (Billie Dee, Denzel, Terrence) and . . . and . . . . Well I can't do more than three fine men at a time. I'm just kidding. This man was handsome as all get out and his skin was so smooth that if his face was on the cover of a magazine you could touch it and feel the silk. I was mesmerized. Not realizing what I was doing I stood up from the barstool and my face was in his chest. I felt my head move slowly upward until my eyes met his and I asked, "Could I please have another Malibu Bay Breeze?" He gave me a slight grin and said, "Sure, I'll be right back." My girlfriend Jakee tugged at the back of my blouse and whispered to me, "Girl, sit your ass down. You are looking very desperate."

Nine. I didn't normally go there more than once a month with my girls but now that my husband was so occupied with his under the cover lover I had free time on my hands. He was still living at the house because he was thinking that cheaper to keep her logic. Well we all know that anything worth having comes with a price. And he was going to pay big time. I finished typing the last of my notes for the Friday meeting and shut down my computer. I stretched and let out a long and loud sigh. It was time for me to do some real work. I grabbed my purse and jacket and while whistling, *'Don't you worry be happy,'* I sashayed my happy little ass to the elevator. When the doors opened my husband was standing there. All I could think was damn, damn and more damn!

"What are you doing here Darryl?"

He shifted his body and gave me that I am not in the mood look. "I am suppose to take the Lexus to the shop today. You asked me to pick it up here so we could exchange vehicles. You aren't losing your mind are you?" he said laughing.

I retorted, "Oh no I lost that when I said I do," smiling back at him.

A frown formed on his face.

"Look don't start because I am doing you a favor," he said pointing his finger at me.

The elevator went down and when the doors opened I angrily walked past him and I threw my hand up and tossed him my keys.

"I've got things and people to do." As I walked in between the revolving doors I heard him yell. "Whattt?!"

I laughed and thought to myself, he's joking right? We exchanged vehicles and a few other not so kind comments and he was on his way. I was sure that his little honey would get to ride in my Lexus before it was brought back to me. But it was all right because his Navigator was going to get a little humpty-hump action itself. I decided to stop by one of my favorite stores Sexy and No Secrets. The store truly did live up to its name. I had purchased things from there before that had left Darryl speechless and with his tongue hanging out. That gave me a thought. I would leave the bag and the receipt in his Navigator. Cha-ching!!!! And ladies I'm using his MasterCard. I never leave home without it. I know he buys his new flavor of the month one or two things. I am not mad. That's why I buy four or five things when I shop with his card. After about an hour I had finished shopping and walked back to the Navigator and headed home. Once I was home I went into the bathroom and took a long hot shower. Just as I was about to step out my cell phone rang. It was my girl Jakee.

"Hey bffl." You caught me getting out of the shower. What's going on?"

She told me that she would not be able to hang out at the Club Nine because they were sending her on an overnight flight to Boston. I was disappointed but I understood work is work. I told her to have a safe flight and not to do anything that I wouldn't do and hung up. Before I could walk away from the phone it rang again. This time it was my girl Shayna.

"Hey Shayna I just hung up with Jakee. She can't hang with us tonight, I told her."

"That's why I am calling, I can't make it either." Starting to get a little attitude in my voice I asked her, "And why not?" I guess she picked up on my attitude because I could feel her neck rolling through the receiver, "Because the twins are sick. They have the freaking chicken pox!"

I softened my tone but still disappointed I said, "I am sorry to hear that. Give them each a hug for me and tell them I will bring them some things to keep them entertained tomorrow."

"I will and I love you girl."

I hung the phone up and contemplated whether or not I should go alone. I came to the conclusion it would be better if I did because neither Jakee nor Shayna would approve of my behavior because they knew that I was not over Darryl. I knew it too. But this was not about getting over or getting even. Who was I trying to kid? It was about getting even. And I knew the risks that would be involved but I was not going to turn back now. So I went into my walk-in closet and examined my surplus of shoes. Selecting my shoes first would help me choose my outfit. The red stiletto heels were the choice I made. And to compliment them was the tightest, slinkiest and shortest black dress that I had in my wardrobe. I did a little twirl in front of the full-length mirror and looking over my shoulder at my nicely rounded behind I smiled. With my red clutch in hand I grabbed my three-quarter-length coat and keys and headed out to the parked Navigator. Once inside I decided to call and annoy Darryl but I also wanted to make sure that he was coming home tonight. I knew that he would be up pacing and watching the clock waiting for me to come in. I was never one to stay out very late especially without calling. I pulled up to the Club Nine and the valet came around and opened the door. As I started to step out I noticed that his eyes were wandering further and further up my legs.

"Excuse me little wolf don't climb up the branches unless you intend to play in the bush."

The look on his face told me that he was embarrassed and inexperienced so I let him know that it was all right and he apologized. There was no harm done. In fact I thought it was quite flattering. Once I was inside Club Nine I spotted Sweet tea at the bar. I was going to have to find out his real name. For all I knew maybe it was Sweet tea. I went to the bar and he immediately said, "It is going to be a very long night."

Looking at him inquisitively I asked, "And just what do you mean by that?"

He grinned and said with the snap of his fingers.

"Because girrrrl the way you look in that dress all of the brothers up in here are going to be buying you drinks all night long. But I am not mad at you because every time they drop a dime I get to bend over and pick it up. And honey some of these brothers won't mind me bending over. So I am going to get laid and paid."

All I could do was laugh. I asked Sweet tea about the waiter who had been there the previous night. He told me that his name was Jonathan and that he did not have a girlfriend at the time. He also said that Jonathan was a huge flirt. Just the critique I needed to hear. The game was about to be put into play. Jonathan was scheduled to be at the club at ten o'clock. It was now nine fifty-nine. I watched as the minute hand swept around the clock. Ten o'clock on the nose and in he walked. He was hot as hell. The devil himself he was. He had a smile on his face as his eyes searched the room for young, sultry flesh. He stopped once or twice to whisper in a couple of ears. I was actually jealous. He came my way and I pretended that I had not noticed him. Then I felt his warm breath on the side of my neck.

"You don't have to pretend I saw you looking tonight and last night. You have two choices. One you can stand up and slap my face and have me fired or two you can meet me in thirty minutes."

"You are very observant and very bold. You are not working tonight?" I asked as calmly as I could.

He bluntly said, "No, I came here for you. You are on fire."

Trying not to turn red I said, "Oh and I guess you are going to put it out?"

He chuckled and then placing his lips as close to my ear as he could get he said slow and with confidence,

"No I intend on stirring the flames. You will need the fire department to put out what I start. Thirty minutes and I will see you out front."

His tongue flicked across the tip of my ear lobe and I suddenly had to press my thighs together. I looked up and Sweet tea was looking at me. I had a blank expression on my face. Sweet tea's expression had that look that said, "Uh-huh what are you going to do now?"

I stood up from the bar and tugged at my dress, then took one last sip of my drink and said to Sweet tea, "It's on."

Sweet tea smiled and gave me three snaps and said, "You go Miss Thang' and call me if you need some help."

I stopped dead in my tracks and looked at Sweet tea with a look that could kill. Was this brother Jonathan on the DL?

Sweet tea picking up my drift waved his hand in the air and said, "No he's straight I was just kidding."

I went outside and Jonathan was there talking to the valet. I was going to send for the Navigator but Jonathan stopped me.

"No we will walk."

I looked puzzled for a minute but then I said, "Okay."

We walked about two and a half blocks. I had not realized how beautiful and picturesque the neighborhood was. It was quite romantic. There was

Pulling at the fabric that covered her nipples she sucked her teeth and said aloud, "Small and perky just right for the picking." She sprayed herself lavishly with her favorite perfume and then she slipped her feet into her five-inch stilettos. She stood in front of the mirror and checked to make sure that all was well and intacked before she gave herself the thumbs up. She removed the terry cloth towel from her head and a mound of curls fell forward and danced about her face. She walked into the bathroom dragging the towel behind her and tossed it into the hamper as she walked past it. She removed the can of mousse from the shelf and sprayed a tablespoon amount in one of her hands and rubbed it through her curls. Sitting the can down on the corner of the sink she briskly ran the fingers of both of her hands through her curls adding more volume and bounce. She loved her hair being natural and after months of deep conditioning it was becoming chemical free. She smiled at herself. Yes she was happy with what she saw and leaning forward she spoke softly into the mirror, "Thank you God for I know that there is better but I also know that there is worse. I am thankful for being placed somewhere in the middle." Jordan was thankful that she was happy with herself. That she had that confidence that let her be who she wanted to be. No one could define her.

LAYING DOWN THE LAW

Jordan wrapped the towel around her freshly shampooed hair and walked over to her bed. She sat on the edge of the queen-sized mattress and propped both of her feet onto the cushioned ottoman that sat at the foot of it. She squeezed the bottle of cocoa butter lotion until she had an ample amount in the palm of her hand. Rubbing her palms together she then smoothed the creamy mixture onto her long and shapely left leg. She repeated the steps and did the same to her other leg. She lifted one leg up into the air and pointed her toes. Tilting her head from side to side she admired her leg. She thought that her legs were her best attribute next to her hazel eyes of course. She was not as well endowed in the breast department as she would have liked but she would never think of having implants put in. To each their own but it was just not for her. She may have been small but she was healthy and still getting laid on the regular. Which led her to believe that having large breasts were not as important as they were made out to be unless you were a baby of course. She finished smothering her body with the rich cocoa butter and slid into her frayed Jean shorts and her black racer back tee-top.

mostly jazz music that was coming from the clubs and restaurants that we passed by as we walked. We walked until we entered into a park filled with trees and shrubbery. Jonathan took my hand and led me to an out of the way spot in the park that was heavily surrounded by thick shrubbery. He pulled me to him and the next thing I knew I felt his tongue dancing in my mouth. I had no time to think or to react. I just gave into the passion. You would have thought that neither of us had been in a sexual encounter in years. I was close to that, but as fine as this single man was I just knew that he did the do on a regular basis. I felt his hands begin to raise my hemline higher and higher. It was already short so he didn't have too far to go. I was amazed at myself. I was totally out of control. I didn't know that I could moan and move and move and moan. Oh hell I can't explain it. I was calling his name and the more I did the more he was satisfying me. Totally fulfilled and exhausted I looked at him and said, "An Angel must have sent you to me."

He kissed me on my lips and then zipped his pants up and with the cockiest grin on his face he said,

"No your husband did."

was three months into their relationship before they became sexually intimate. Jordan set the terms and even though Troy felt that he was under a contract he was patient and she grew to love and trust him. But even still she felt uneasy about giving up control even in the bedroom. Troy had been a detective for only eight months and it was all still new to him but that did not keep his ego from becoming a little large. Their first night of intense sex he wanted to lay down the law. Or at least he had tried to. She remembered how her detective Troy Bennett read her rights as he had her handcuffed to his bedpost. He was hovered over her with his erect penis pressing into her thigh just inches away from her lollipop. That's what Troy had nicknamed it and even though she tried to convince him that she did not like the name she was turned on by it. In fact whenever one of her friends would ask her what she was going to give Troy for any special occasion she would respond, "Lollipop." Then she would smile as she thought of how he would always whisper in her ear whenever she would arouse him, "I can't wait to lick my lollipop." So after three months he would have to wait no longer. He held her shoulders and pushed her back onto his bed. He placed his knee between hers and shoved at them and ordered her in his husky voice to, "Spread um." He

He uncuffed her and she slapped him. He slapped her back and he threw her back onto the bed. Her heart began to race because she did not know what magnitude of anger he had risen to. He hovered over her again and this time he leaned forward and he looked her in her face. He got as close as he could until his breath was hers and then he kissed her gently. He whispered in her ear, "You want control then take it." Jordan reached up and threw her arms around his neck and flipping him over onto his back she mounted him. She reached for his right hand and placed the handcuff that was still attached to the bedpost around his wrist. She did the same with his other wrist. She felt his thick penis between her thighs but she was not ready to ride her stallion. She kissed his neck and licked his nipples. She massaged his chest as she placed small nibbles down his rippled stomach. She placed her tongue at the base of his penis and licked it all the way up to the tip. She took his tip into her mouth and teased him for a moment and then she licked him down to the base again. She did this several times but each time taking him deeper into her mouth when she would reach the tip. Troy was packing and he wanted to enter her and release all of his explosives inside of her. He tried to reach for her but the handcuffs had him restrained. She continued to toy her scream out his name but instead Jordan rode him and she rode him hard until she could hear the handcuffs continuously clanging against the metal of the bedposts. She picked up the key and threw it to the floor. Troy growled out like a beast. She knew that he wanted to be released so that he could touch her and kiss her, to fondle her breasts, to slap her on her ass and to grab her hips so that he could push deeper inside of her. But he could do none of those things because Jordan was once again in control and she loved laying down the law—a.k.a. Detective Troy Bennett.

SECRETS

The room was filled with laughter and good spirits. It felt good to be home and among all of my girlfriends. So much had happened to each one of us in the past year that we had all been apart. We all had our own individual lives that we led and each came with there own drama and stories to tell. As I looked around the room I admired all of the shades of beauty that created a kaleidoscope of hues and colors. What a lovely garden Heaven must be with all of the African ancestors that had preceded us in death. A garden filled with spiritual petals from the darkest shades of ebony to the lightest hint of ivory. I myself will add the hues of cinnamon and caramel to the Lords garden when He chooses to call me home. There is nothing more exhilarating then to walk into a room filled with women of color who have it together, getting it together and who are putting it together. That's why three years ago my cousin Renee and I decided to form a Sistahs Only Club. We wanted women of color who wanted to share their creativity, emotions, aspirations, dreams and secrets to have a place to come together. So we began to network with our girlfriends that we knew from elementary school through college. We came together as a group once a year. The only stipulations were that you had to be at least fifty and you could not pass judgement. We often view this age as the defining point in our lives known as the infamous halfway mark. For many of us it truly is the beginning of our lives. After raising children, taking care of our ailing parents, financial woes and dealing with unfaithful spouses we finally take a good look at ourselves. Fifty is the age to give yourself not necessarily a new beginning but a new look at what you want and where you want to be in your life. As a group, we planned activities and jointly shared the financial responsibility. This meant there was no such thing as, I can't go because I don't have the funds. There was never a missing pea in the pod. We often took cruises or flew to exotic places and just pampered ourselves with sun and tropical drinks. If we happened to fall in love with romance we did that too and we obliged each other with the saying, "What's done in Vegas—stays in Vegas." Some of us were all right with the idea of having a fling but then there were those of us who were appalled at the mere thought. This is why we incorporated the No judgement rule: *You can think what you want, you just can't say it.* Of course there were the signs of disapproval that showed often on faces but the lips remained tightly sealed.

underneath. So I tried to keep going because I would not have felt comfortable sitting in a hotel lobby half naked with people I did not know or wouldn't care to get to know. After passing two more hotels I decided to give in. I was no competition for the wind and the sand. I started walking towards the hotel that was surrounded by skyscraping palm trees. The winds ferocious movement of the leaves of the palm trees led my imagination to believe that they were dancing to the pulsating rhythm of African drums. I continued walking towards the hotel when suddenly I felt hands gripping at my waist. My heart began racing. I tried to pull away but before I could I was swiftly turned in one move. My lips were covered with another pair of lips that muffled my screams. I tried turning my body to put distance between the intruder and myself. His grip was too strong. The rain mixed with my tears. I just wanted to be in the safe comfort of my husband's arms. I stopped fighting and pretended to succumb to the intruder's demands hoping that he would somehow change his mind and not bring harm to me. When he felt as though I were giving up he loosened his grip. I wanted to run but instinct told me that this would not be a good choice. Instead I told myself to try to reason with him. My heart was beating so hard I knew that he could hear it. Blinking the rain and tears away from my eyes I was astonished to find the identity of the eyes that were starring back at me. They were the eyes of my husband. I stuttered to get the words out. I was angry because he had frightened me but relieved at the same moment to find that I was not in harms way. He saw my fear and cradled me in his arms. His arms slowly dropped from around my shoulders to my waist. I felt the palms of his hands caress my buttocks. He pressed my body to him until I could feel his manhood. He slowly kissed my neck and chin then bringing his lips to mine kissing me with a passion I had long missed and been yearning for. I needed to take a breath. I needed to rationalize what was going on. The palm trees, the wind and the sand were all silent and still in my mind. What was about to happen in this not so well hidden place? I felt him move his body and sensations began to stir within me. I was about to have an affair with my husband. He was allowing me to unleash all passion that I had read about and had dreamed about. The quiet storm that had laid dormant in our marriage was about to emerge. I was trying not to be overly excited because I did not want him to know that my expectations may have been too high. I knew that there could not be failure. If he felt that he had not delivered we would never be able to move beyond this point. Every move been taking you for granted. I became selfish in my thinking that I would be the only man to look at you or to want you in such a way. I knew that if he found you before I did I would be the one to lose." Then he said with such honesty, "I love you."

I held onto my husband tightly and without looking at him I knew that he was crying. We had opened a new chapter in our life, our marriage and most importantly in our intimacy. We no longer needed to keep secrets about our desires, our passion or our needs. The sound of the microphone echoed bringing me back into the room. Number fourteen was being asked to step up to the podium. I would be called next. Lucky number fifteen. I smiled to myself as I tried to select the Sistahs in the room who would gasp when I told them that I had an affair. There would be quite a few. Eventually I will tell them that it was with my husband, but until then it is my secret.

PATIENCE IS A VIRTUE

The alarm clock sounded and she heard Charles curse as he slapped the nightstand instead of the snooze button. She mumbled under her breath as she had done the previous mornings that had begun the same way for the last four months. She felt the covers fall back against her as he shoved his way out of their bed and shuffled his feet towards the bathroom. And as usual he forgot to close the door before turning on the light. She ducked her head under the covers and cursed him but her language was a little more offensive than what he had yelled earlier. His routine was so clockwork that she knew that it was useless to try to fall back to sleep because he was insensitive to all of the noise that he would be making. She had tried to approach him in a non-aggressive manner asking him to be a little more considerate. Reminding him that not everyone has to be an early worm but obviously he had no idea of what it meant to be quiet or it could have been that he just did not give a damn. She waited until she heard the door slam shut and the key turn the lock and she drifted back to sleep. When she awakened sometime around ten she washed her face and brushed her teeth and put on a pair of sweatpants and a tee shirt and went for a quick run through the neighborhood. It was a gorgeous day and the sun and the light breeze felt great against her skin. She ran her daily route and waved a friendly good morning as she passed a few of the neighbors who were out planting and watering their lawns. It was a beautiful neighborhood and she and Charles had lived there for over fifteen years. That was about half of their married life. She remembered the first day that they had moved in. Charles had surprised her and gone to the house earlier that afternoon and he had created for her a private garden. He had placed well over ten dozen bouquets of different flowers all through the house. A mixture of petals laced the floor as they led to the rug that lay in front of the fireplace. He had candles lit and champagne chilling. It all had taken her breath away just as the lovemaking that they did in that very moment in front of their new fireplace. The warmth of the fire as the flames danced about them as Charles smothered her naked body with kisses. The champagne that was never drunk from their glasses he drizzled over her body and then removed it from all of the right places with his tongue. Pouring it between her breasts making a little river that flowed down to her valley. He placed his tongue there and he caught the drops that soon mixed with her wetness. Once he did reassure her that everything would resume to normal once it was over, so she agreed to be a bit more patient. So after she removed her sweaty clothing she went to her vanity and opened the drawer and took out her Monday vibrator. She had one for each day of the week. They were each a different color, size and they all did different functions. She believed that no two men were the same so why should her vibrators be the same? She sat in the chair and placed each of her legs over an arm. She scooted her hips forward a little so that she was in a comfortable position. She turned the vibrator on low speed and inserted it into her moist vagina increasing the speed as she felt her orgasm climaxing. She squeezed her breasts as she imagined Charles standing there watching her while she pleasured herself physically and him visually. She switched the vibrator control to maximum speed and as she felt the pounding and intense pulsation between her walls she threw her head back against the chair and she screamed his name, "Charles, Charles, Oh God Charles!" She sat there for a moment to regain her compose. She removed the vibrator and squeezed her thighs together tightly to make sure that she had received all of her orgasm. She then went to shower. She had not eaten any breakfast so she was famished and headed downstairs to make herself

49

Now she was curious and questioned whether she had read the date wrong. She kept going over it in her mind and then she decided to just call the restaurant. When she called she asked if they did in fact have a reservation for two. The answer was yes and it was for Mr. and Mrs. Charles Bayne. She thanked the gentleman on the phone and hung up. Now she was really puzzled. She was Mrs. Bayne so who in the hell was he taking, she asked herself. She did not want to jump to any conclusions so there was only one way to find out. She would go to the restaurant and wait for him. At six o'clock that evening she called for a taxi and when it arrived she instructed the driver to take her to the Oyster Point Restaurant. She waited until she saw her husband's vehicle drive up to the valet. He got out dressed to the nines and when the valet pulled away in his car he was locked arm in arm with a young woman who could have been their daughter. He placed his hand under her chin and lightly kissed her on the lips. The shock of it all left her speechless and motionless. She sat there in the taxi until she heard the driver ask, "Excuse me Miss are you okay? Are you getting out?" She looked at him as if she had no idea what he was talking about and then she told him, "No, no I am not getting out. Can you please take me

Danny turned to her, "Oh hey Mrs. Bayne. I just passed him in the hallway on my way down. I think he still has one more patient. I heard him tell someone he would be right back. That husband of yours works too hard."

She smiled at Danny and told him to have a good night. She went up to Charles' office and placed her ear to the door. She could hear faint whispering so she knocked and then tried to turn the knob but the door was locked. Charles yelled out, "Who is it!?"

"It's me honey your wife, Patience," she said as sexy and as coy as she could under the circumstances. She heard a little scuffling and then he came and opened the door. There was sweat on his brow. Patience asked him, "Charles are you alright, you look a little overwhelmed?"

He looked at her and cleared his throat, "Yes, yes-but what are you doing here?"

She looked at him and smiled, "What a wife can't surprise her husband? You are always surprising me so I thought that I would do a little something for you."

Patience opened her coat and she was now standing in front of him naked as a J-bird with the exception of her five-inch stilettos. Charles did not know what to do or to say. Patience pushed him back against his desk and she was not going to take no for an answer. She had his pants and drawers down and around his ankles before he could do anything. He tried to stop her but he fumbled and lost his balance falling backwards onto the desktop. Patience climbed on top of him ready to mount him.

He grabbed her and shouted, "No Patience, no!"

Patience stood up and pulled her coat closed and she turned her head towards the bathroom door and yelled, "You can bring your skinny little ass out now because I know that you are in there."

She looked back at Charles.

Charles sat up straight on the desk and asked her, "Whom are you talking too. Have you gone crazy or something?"

Patience fixed her eyes on Charles and repeated it again but this time she added, "Patience is my name and not my demeanor right at this time so you might not want me to come in there and get your ass!"

This time she heard the knob turn and the door opened. It was the same girl that she had seen him with for the past few weeks. Patience put her hands on her hips and asked her, "Shouldn't you be in school or something?"

Then she stepped closer to Charles and she slapped the hell out of him.

She looked at him with defiance and with no uncertain terms she told him, "I have been following you for three weeks hoping that you would come to your senses and end this little fling. Patience is a virtue Charles, but Patience isn't stupid."

She pulled the folded piece of paper from her pocket and shoved it at him informing him as she pressed it into his chest, "You can call my attorney in the morning from your office or from her house whichever you choose to take up residency."

Patience then turned and looked at the other woman and shook her head. She walked past her wanting to tear into her but she kept her composure until she was on the other side of the door. Her face flooded with tears and her heart filled with pain she walked down the long corridor to return home alone.

ROUND TWO

Like a candle that burns
with a wicked flame
he made me hot each
time he whispered my
name the warm wax that
trickled down between
my legs had me in heat
like a dog I begged

each and every stoke sent
a shiver down my spine
he wanted to bring me to
Heaven
I wasn't ready so I
declined

my back arched like
the golden gate bridge
knowing I didn't want to
climax but I was nearing
the ridge

his eyes locked into mine
and a message was sent
he knew he had me where
I wanted to be my moans
of satisfaction gave him
the hint

he was like dark
chocolate thunder that
hovered over me from
above and I saw all the
colors of the rainbow
as he rode through my
tunnel of love

our rhythm like music slow
at first then picking up the
pace never missing a beat
deepening our embrace

gently he kissed me as
his body rose and then
fell giving and taking all
he could stand no more I
could tell

so locking him into my love
I held onto him tight
sending his body into a
frenzy he was done for
the night

his breathing so heavy he
could not speak
I knew he wanted to
thank me but I had left
him weak

placing my hand on his
cheek and suckling his
lower lip
I slowly lowered my head
until I found the tip

offering what he could
not resist doing what he
needed me to do stroking
his head and his ego we
were ready for Round two.

RE-MIX

The party was out of control and so was I. The Deejay at the Club Re-mix was mixing all of the right sounds and my body was in overdrive. The crowd was in a mad frenzy and it didn't matter who you came to the party with because everybody was trying to get their freak on. I was moving and shaking my derriere when this fine specimen of a man found his way into my space. We locked eyes for a minute and then it was on. I raised my arms in the air and moved in closer to him moving my hips until they were matched with his. He placed his hands in the well of my back and pulled me closer. I felt him and he felt me. I turned my body around so that his manhood was now pressing against my perfectly rounded ass. We danced in perfect rhythm and the message that I was sending let him know that this was not going to be our only dance. By the time the song had ended we were both glistening in sweat. He took my hand and led me through the crowd to the bar. And with the gorgeous smile that landscaped his face he asked me, "What's your pleasure?"

I looked at him and wickedly let my eyes fall down to the bulge in his perfectly fitting designer jeans. He placed a finger under my chin and raised my head until we were both looking at one another.

"I was referring to a drink."

I laughed and tilted my head to the side and giving him a wink I told him, "I know what you meant but that doesn't change what I was thinking. It was just too easy to resist. If you're buying I'll have a glass of White Zinfandel to start."

He gave me this inquisitive look and asked, "To start?"

I laughed again and replied, "The night is still young and if my intuition is right we will be spending at least another hour or two together. But you let me know if I am wrong."

He looked at me, shook his head and laughed. He called out to the bartender and shaking his head again looked at me and smiled. We sat at the bar and after two more drinks we were both feeling a little mellow. He told me that his name was Jayden and that he was a self-employed mechanic.

So I teased him by asking, "So you are good with your hands?"

Just when he was about to respond the Dee-Jay played a song that must have been one of his favorites because the next thing that I knew I was being led back onto the dance floor. As I was being guided through the crowd I couldn't help but smile as I noticed the women looking at me enviously. Look on divas because you will not be in my shoes. Not tonight anyway. They must have caught what I was thinking because I swear I heard one of them call me a BITCH! But sometimes that is what you have to be to get what you want. The man had it going on and my chassis needed to be oiled and primed. He was built like a locomotive and it was my intent to ride him from the engine to the caboose. We found our space on the floor and I began moving my body to the rhythm of the music making sure that each movement was as seductive as the next. At one point Jayden stopped dancing and just stood there and watched. If he had been sitting down he would have been paying for a lap dance. I smiled to myself because I knew that I did have that on my agenda. He got himself together and put his arms around my waist and pulled me closer to him. I had hooked him because he eyeballed the room letting all of the other men know that I had been claimed. The song ended and the Deejay slipped into an old school slow jam. Everybody latched onto their partners and all of a sudden it was as if we were in the basement at a house party back in the day. There was a lot of grinding going on and Jayden and I was in the middle of it all. I couldn't get close enough to him. The more I pushed into him the tighter he grabbed my assets. I felt him lean in and kiss my neck. When he went in for the second time I turned my head and our lips met for a moment. We paused and looked at each other. I moistened my lips with my tongue and before I could put it back into my mouth he was kissing me. His kiss came with a message. It was loud and clear asking me if I wanted this. And believe me I wanted it. I wanted it bad. I took Jayden by the hand and led him off of the dance floor. We walked to the elevator that led to the parking garage. Once inside the elevator we kissed passionately as though we were trying to suck the air out of our lungs. We intimately touched each other. My hands caressed his manhood while his hands found their way beneath my dress and fondled my breasts. The elevator came to a stop but we didn't. Jayden pulled the spaghetti straps to my dress down over my shoulders until my breasts were fully exposed.

I tensed a little because my breasts were moderate in size and he sensed my being uncomfortable.

He cupped them in his hands and said, "They are beautiful just like the woman that they belong to." Then he kissed and suckled each one. I could have cried but he was making it hard for me to stay focused. I didn't know if I would see Jayden again but I wanted to leave him with a message that said I was not just a woman but a GOOD woman. I didn't know what he was thinking. Maybe he was hoping that I would be his freak of the week and he had no intentions other then getting laid. But whatever he was thinking I was going to love him right. I gently pushed Jayden away from me and adjusted my dress and pressed the button for the elevator doors to open. I took his hand and led him to my car.

He looked at me as if surprised and asked, "This is you?" as he pointed at my car. He seemed impressed to see the black sport convertible Mercedes.

I chuckled, "Every hard earn dollar of it."

I tossed him my keys and told him to drive. We drove through town with the top down and took in the cool night air. I placed his hand on my thigh and gave him a wink. He knew exactly what to do. I laid my head back on the soft Italian leather as he fondled me. His fingers moved at the right pace and touched all of the right spots. By this time I had my right leg hanging over the door and I was wide open. My fingers joined in with his and I was on the verge of climax when we pulled into the driveway of my townhouse. I moaned as I felt the tightness between my thighs. I hit the garage door opener and just as it was going down so was Jayden. I screamed with pleasure as his tongue swirled around and around on my clitoris. I was beginning to feel the uncomfortable position in my back so I had to let myself go. I let him take me over the edge screaming his name at every point. I pushed him back into the driver's seat and unzipped his pants and immediately found his manhood. All I heard him say was, "Oh shit, oh shit, oooooh shitttttt!" I lifted my head to find Jayden panting and speechless. We made our way out of the car and into the townhouse. I told him to make himself comfortable and to pour us both a glass of wine. I went up to the bathroom and made a bubble bath in the Jacuzzi tub. I yelled down to Jayden to come up as I began lighting the scented candles that were around the tub. When Jayden walked in he said, "Wow this is nice. This is real nice." I hit the remote for a little jazz music and I sat him down on the chair. I began to strip for him and then I teased him with a lap dance. I was surprised at myself because I was giving the performance of a lifetime. I had just met this man and I had fallen for him. It didn't feel like lust. I felt that he was supposed to have been there. Jayden grabbed me stopping my hips in mid motion. He didn't speak for a moment and I became uneasy.

I asked him, "Is something wrong?"

He shook his head no and said, "No you're a beautiful woman and I am feeling you. I know we just met and you don't really know who I am but I don't want this to be just one night and if that's how it is for you I need to leave now. I didn't come to the club tonight for a bootie-pick up. Not that I am calling you a trick or anything but you know how it is."

I didn't want to act like a silly schoolgirl so instead I looked him in the eye and I said jokingly, "You interrupted the best lap dance of your life for this serious shit. Okay here it is. The 411. No I am not a trick. I am gainfully employed. I work hard, I save hard and I play hard. I know what I want and a one-night stand is not it."

And with that said I threw my arms around his neck and he lifted me carrying me to the bed. He kissed me passionately not skipping a beat as he removed his shirt.

He kissed me again and said, "I'm going to show you how I like to dance."

He kissed every inch of my body. I was so moist and he was so damn good. By the time he entered me I already knew this was going to be everything I had imagined. I knew that what went on in the car was only the appetizer. I was about to get a deluxe meal. He grabbed my hips and moved my body with slow in and out thrusts. Every spot he touched sent my body into spasms. The way he suckled my breasts caressed my shoulders, kissed my neck and Ooh! Oh yeah that's the spot! His thrusts became faster and harder until we both screamed out each other's names.

He kissed my ear lobe and whispered, "I told you I liked to dance."

With that I hit the remote on the CD player and flipped him over onto his back and we began the Re-mix.

HOMEBOY

Adrienne pushed the covers away from her body and swung her legs from the bed to the floor. She could not imagine what fool would be cutting grass at this hour of the morning. It seemed as if she had just gotten into her bed from the birthday party she had attended that previous night. Her head was pounding and the buzz of the lawnmower was not helping the situation. She went immediately to the window with all intent to throw about a few curse words at whoever had awakened her from her much needed sleep. She raised the blinds and just as she was about to open the window she looked down and saw a very fine specimen of a man. He had on a pair of denim jeans with a dingy white rag hanging from his back pocket. He was not wearing a shirt, which exposed his upper body. His skin was smooth and his back was moist with perspiration. His muscles bulged at his sides as he bent over to pull away the sticks and rocks that had gotten caught in the mower. Adrienne lowered the blinds and peeked through one of the slats as she waited for him to turn around. She wanted to see the face that went along with this muscular body. She waited with anticipation but also with doubt. She doubted that he would be anything worth looking at because if the body was fine the face was almost always disappointing. She slapped herself on the wrist for being so shallow but she was who she was. He turned and her mouth fell open. She could not believe her eyes. It was Stephen a.k.a. "Little Stevie." She was shocked and questioned in her mind, "When did he grow up?" Even though he was younger than she was, as children they had always played together. She had even babysat for him on a few occasions but she did not remember him being that attractive. At least not attractive enough to look how he did now. She remembered him as being scrawny and uncoordinated. As they grew into teenagers her girlfriends would comment on his dimples and his great smile but she just looked at him as the kid next door who she played with and teased a lot. Now she was starring at him in disbelief. He had grown into a tall, cool, thirst quenching glass of water and she devilishly thought how she would love to drink from his spout anytime. She raised the blinds again and this time she opened the window. She yelled out to him, "Hey homeboy!"

He could not hear her over the lawnmower so she waited until he turned around again. She put her arm out of the window and waved at him and yelled out again, "Hey homeboy!"

He glanced up and seeing her he turned the lawnmower off. He took the rag from his back pocket and wiped the sweat from his face.

He yelled up to her, "Hey, what's up homey? Long time no see."

They both smiled at one another and childhood memories floated through the air.

Adrienne responded back, "Yeah it has been a minute. I see you still have that big head of yours."

He laughed and adjusting his pants at the waist he replied, "Yeah but which one are you talking about? Oh my bad, unfortunately you have only seen one."

Adrienne opened her mouth as if she were totally shocked at his comment then she said, "Yeah still a big head," then she closed the window and let the blinds down. She stood by the window and peeked through the blinds a little longer. She smiled and thought, "Maybe I will get to see the other big head." After all she had seen it before when they were children. She went to the phone and dialed her girlfriend Tracey's number. Tracey had always tried to coax Adrienne to have a relationship with Stephen but he was just too young and too close for Adrienne's comfort zone. But they were no longer little playmates. In Adrienne's mind she wanted a big playmate and she may have just found out that the boy next door might just be the swing she needed. When Tracey answered she immediately gave her the 411. By the time the conversation had ended they had already plotted a scheme to get Stephen hooked. Adrienne went back to the window and peered out but Stephen had gone. She went back to her bed and lay across the crumpled sheets. Her hair fell softly about the satin pillow and her body tensed as she felt his hand move slow and gentle up her leg. She moaned as she felt his breath behind her knee where he placed a tender kiss before proceeding to her inner thigh. Lingering there for a moment before he planted a garden of small kisses that released an ache in her vagina. She licked her upper lip with the tip of her tongue as she anticipated his tongue coming to satisfy her ache. But he did not rush to satisfy her. He only came close enough so that she could feel his hot and heavy breath that teased her. She needed to feel something against her body so she reached down with her hand to touch herself but he stopped her. Their eyes met and he shook his head no. He wanted to be in control. She moaned as if in agony and let her head return to the satin pillow. She let him have control. He reached for her other leg and repeating what he had done with the other he stopped once again just as she felt his breath at her opening. He was torturing her. She cupped her breasts and pulled at her nipples. Then remembering he had control she looked to him for his approval. He did not speak nor did he stop her so she continued to taunt her nipples until they were erect and plump. He placed her legs one at a time over each of his shoulders and kissed her from her lower belly to her engorge clitoris. His kisses were light and faint to the touch, which made her arch her back. She strained her lower body to reach his tongue and he toyed with her almost pushing her to frustration. She let her buttocks fall back onto the bed and without giving any notice he placed his mouth fully onto her clit and sucked. The sensation forced Adrienne to yell up to Heaven and she reached down and held the back of his head so that he would not move away. She moved her hips and holding onto him as tightly as she could she begged for him not to stop. Not following her command he grabbed her hands and pinning them down to the bed he released them so that he could feel the mixture of pleasure and pain. She repeated the scenario until he stopped her. They were both drenched in each other's sweat and passion. He eased out of her mouth and looking deep into her eyes he took her hands once again and he entered her. She felt him glide through her moistness and as he pulled back each time and pushed a little further she felt him swell. They moaned, "Ohhh" in unison. Their rhythm was slow and steady. He kissed her mouth. She suckled his lower lip. He kissed her once again and she whispered, "Fuck me, fuck me Stephen." His buttocks rose and he pushed into her walls and his body now moving fast and hard he rode her. She held on and as her climax came closer she squeezed her muscles to receive it all. She pushed her hips forward and . . . . Bang! Bang! Adrienne sat up in the bed and looked around the room. She grabbed her head and tried to focus. She heard the noise again, "Bang! Bang!" Someone was banging on her front door. Her shirt was halfway unbuttoned and her pants were twisted as if she had been in a cat fight. She got herself together and realized that she had fallen asleep and had been dreaming. Now she was really pissed off not just because they were banging the hell out of her front door but because they had interrupted her getting banged. She hated having a good wet dream position and I stood frozen in my tracks waiting to be cursed out and sent home. I tried to spit out an apology but I was numb. I waited patiently for him to verbalize my punishment but instead he turned slowly and looking at me with a blank expression said nothing. My eyes met his for a fleeting moment and then they went to the floor. I managed to mumble, "I'm so sorry," through my embarrassment. He did not say anything, but his silence felt that much worse. He turned and left the room. I helped the other staff clean up the mess that was made and refilled the tray with more drinks. I really did not want to go back out there after the incident but I still had two hours of serving left to do. I pulled myself together and made my entrance back into the room and hoped that no one noticed my nervousness. The hands on the clock were just not moving fast enough. I sucked in my breath and made another sweep around the room. There was a group of people in a circle engrossed in a conversation. I approached to offer them drinks and the minute I said, "Excuse me," he turned around and I felt my hand quiver beneath the tray. He must have sensed it because he placed his hand on my wrist to steady the tray. I nodded and prayed that they would take the drinks quickly so that I would not make a fool out of myself again. Everyone seemed to be satisfied with the drinks except one. Of course there is always one who just has to be different. She took a sip from the glass of champagne and she proceeded to speak. I was not certain if her comment was directed at me or to the host. She looked over her designer glasses and asked, "Did the help drink up all of the good liquor or are you saving it for different clientele Andrew?" She was starring at me as if she was waiting for me to respond. I gave her an empty look to fill up her obviously empty head and walked away. Even I knew that this was the best champagne. I had been the one to sign the invoice when it was delivered. I heard her whisper something and then she chuckled. This was my opportunity to send her ass sailing to the other side of the room but I continued to walk away and disappeared into the room of executives and other bimbos. Finally the night had ended and we had just about finished cleaning up and packing the truck with all of the supplies and equipment. My feet and neck were killing me. I had to get these ugly ass shoes off of my feet. I sat on the brick wall that outlined the driveway and removed my shoes. I pulled my right leg up across my left knee and massaged my aching foot. Everyone had packed their belongings and began leaving in their cars. I waved as they rolled passed me. I glanced at my watch and noticed that my ride should waiting for a cab. He came walking towards me and I remembered that I did not have on my shoes and immediately turned to get them from off of the wall. He was now standing in front of me and even though I had seen his face earlier he looked more distinguished and relaxed. He was not so stiff and structured as he had appeared earlier in the day when he was in his tuxedo. His hair was wavy and well kept. He was now wearing a pair of casual shorts and a designer tee that hugged his physique exposing his muscular arms and six packs. He looked on as I struggled to slide my still aching feet that were now slightly swollen back into my shoes. He laughed and said, "Why don't you pick those up and come into the house. You can wait for your cab inside." I welcomed the offer but I declined. I did not want to impose. It was not as if I had been one of his guests. He insisted that I come in for fear that one of his neighbors would eventually call the police. In fact he was surprised that no one had done that already. I agreed to go with him to the house. Once inside with the crowd no longer there I could see how beautiful his home really was. The marble floors the high ceilings with the crown moldings and crystal lighting accentuated by candlelight. I followed him into a sitting room that was quite cozy and warm. The glow from the fireplace gave it a feel of being in work with are assholes and somewhat sticks in the mud but you kept your professionalism intact." I didn't hear anything he said past, "I was watching you." Why was he watching me? Did he think that I might steal something? Looking at his face told me that he had not thought that at all. Maybe he thought that I was interesting. Well why not? I'm cute, sexy and I am educating myself. I had a lot to offer didn't I? He did seem nice and when would I get this type of opportunity again to sit with the elite. He was not filthy rich but the brother wasn't hurting. So I took a chance and I called and cancelled the cab. He went into the kitchen and brought back a tray of fruit and cheese along with crackers. He put them on the table and asked me if that would do or if I would like something heavier to eat. I was starving and I would have eaten anything at that point. He sat down in the chair opposite of me and asked me the usual question. How long had I been serving at parties? I told him that I had served at about five and it was only to help out a friend. I was a receptionist at a local radio station and I was in my second year of college to get my degree in Communications. It was my dream to have my own radio talk show. I had begun College late due to the lack of income but now I was focused and it was full steam ahead. Time seemed to have gotten beautifully and adorned with fresh cut flowers. I don't know what I was expecting but when I saw the good old traditional eggs, bacon, and pancakes I was a happy camper. Halfway through breakfast and adult small talk we were beginning to make little sexual innuendoes. We were flirting with each other and we both liked the feeling. I opened my mouth and tilted my head backwards and let the pancake syrup drizzle onto my tongue. A little too much came out at one time and the excess dribbled down onto the corner of my mouth. Before it could reach my cheek he was there in front of me and with his tongue he licked the syrup from the corner of my mouth. He stood still and waited for my response. I held his face and he then pushed his tongue deeper into my mouth to give me a passionate kiss. Still locked in an embrace I stood up from my chair. He pulled me in closer to him until there was no place for me to go. Our kisses were now hot and heavy and our breathing was the same. Not stopping for air because air was not what we needed he placed his hands under my buttocks and lifted me onto the table. I felt the plates and silverware being pushed from underneath me. His hands came to the front of my blouse and he unbuttoned the first one, then the next one and then he just reached with both would send me over the edge. He unzipped his pants and raised my buttocks up off of the table. I waited for him to remove my panties but he did not. Instead he slid them to the side and placed his tongue on my hot spot. He moved his tongue from side to side, then up and down. Just as I was feeling no pain he stopped and seductively pulled my panties off. He placed his hands under my knees and threw my legs over his shoulders. He positioned himself in the chair and had breakfast all over again. Just as he had covered his pancakes he covered me with syrup and by the time he was finished eating me I was done. My body jerked and spasm in a way that I had never felt before. Just as one orgasm finished another proceeded to follow. I lay on the table feeling divine. He stood and dropped his pants exposing his all. And rising to the occasion he entered me. The moistness of my body made him slide in and out of me with ease. I began to feel tingles and urges all over again. I touched myself because it felt as though he were not enough. I grabbed his buttocks urging him to go deeper and harder. I smacked his buttocks because I needed this stallion to ride me harder to the finish line. He indulged me by thrusting his hardness into me. We found our rhythm and he placed his hands beneath me and I threw my hands mirror showed me all of the reasons why he no longer loved me and if he did not love me than I did not want to love myself. I slipped into a depression and I began an affair with alcohol. Breakfast was champagne and orange juice; lunch was any rum or vodka mixed with pineapple juice. Dinner was a little better because most times I slept through it. However I always managed to wake up in time for a nightcap. That would be anything that was easily accessible from the bar. Passing by the mirror on my way to the kitchen I looked at myself. I looked so old and used up. My hair was starting to show spurts of gray and I noticed age spots and dimples. The sad thing about it all was that I did not know if I was seeing these changes because they were real or if I was seeing them because he had brought my self-esteem to an all time low. I looked down at the cup in my hand and I thought to myself how pathetic. Moving my hand in a circular motion I swirled the yellow orange contents around in the cup and shook my head. I took a drink of what should have been black coffee instead of the champagne and orange juice and swished it around in my mouth as if it were mouthwash before I gulped it down. A tear slowly slid down my face as I asked out loud, "Why doesn't he love me?" I sat there waiting on an answer that I knew would never come. The clock above the stove read two o'clock in the afternoon and I was still in my nightclothes. Everyday was a struggle for me to get out of bed and to put on clothing. I had no where to go and no longer anyone to live for. I sat down at the table and marveled at the beauty of its wood. It was so solid unlike my broken marriage. I glanced up and I saw the image of myself again. This time I saw it in the glass door of the oven. I wondered if I should stick my head inside of it and turn on the gas. I ran my fingers through my hair and grumbled. It felt dry and coarse not to mention that it had not been washed in awhile. I struggled to remember when I had washed it last. Honestly when I had washed myself. Suddenly my crying became uncontrollable. A downpour of emotions danced upon my face. I picked up the cup that was now empty and threw it across the room. I yelled out, "I hate you, I hate you. You said that you would love me forever!" I put my face down on the table and lay in my puddle of tears. I do not know how long I had laid there or when the hands that were on my shoulders had come into the house. Finally the face came into focus. I asked him abruptly, "How did you get in here!" He looked puzzled as if I should not have asked such a question but he responded, "I used my key. How long have you been like this? You look terrible. What is going on with you? I can smell more have loved you." I laughed sarcastically and I asked him, "If you love me and have always loved me what is the problem? Why are we here?" He looked down at the floor again as if his answer were there. This time without looking up he said, "I love you but I am not in love with you." Suddenly there was a tornado raging inside of me. I started swinging and kicking at him. He was trying to restrain me but I had lost control. He placed his hands on my shoulders and as gently as he could manage he pushed me away. I screamed at him telling him to get out. I did not want him to see me cry. I did not want him to see that he had left a wound so deep that I was fearful that I would never heal. He opened the door and as he walked out he said, "I am sorry and even though you do not believe me I do love you." He opened the door and without looking back at me he walked out. I slammed the door shut and my back fell against the door. My legs gave away from beneath me and with my body trembling and weak I slid to the floor. He knocked one last time saying, "I do love you." I heard his footsteps as he made his way down the steps and along the pathway that led to his car. I heard the car door close and then the roar of the engine fade away into the distance. I wrapped my arms tightly around myself and let the tears fall along with the truth that spilled from my lips, "Liar, liar."

THE GOOD HUMOR MAN

It was one hundred and one degrees in the shade, or at least that was how it felt as Laila wiped the perspiration from her forehead and then from her chest. She opened the door to the freezer and she welcomed the quick blast of cold air that mixed with her moist skin. She wished that she could have stood there all afternoon. She removed a Popsicle from the box after precisely choosing the one that was cherry flavored. She placed the cell phone that was resting in the crook of her neck onto the granite countertop and pressed the speaker button.

"Laila what are you doing?" The voice from the phone asked bold and husky.

"I am getting a Popsicle if you don't mind. If someone had not broken my air conditioner I would be cool instead of hot right now."

"How many times do I have to apologize for that? Anyway I like you hot. And last night you were not so worried about your air conditioner when you were calling my name. Now were you?"

Laila sucked her teeth, "Instead of talking about calling your name you should be calling somebody quick and in a hurry to bring me a new air conditioner. I am not playing T.C. it is too hot in here."

Laila licked the Popsicle as it had begun to melt and drip down her hand. She licked a few more times making a loud slurping sound.

"Damn baby, ease up on the sound effects. I sure do wish that I were that Popsicle. It kind of reminds me of last night. You were off the chain." T.C. said teasing her.

Laila huffed into the phone, "T.C. your mind is always on sex. Except for two nights ago. I don't know what you were thinking when you pushed your foot through the front of my air conditioner."

T.C. boasted into the phone once again with conviction, "You might not have known what I was thinking but you know what I was doing. I was doing to you just what you are doing to that Popsicle. I was licking that cherry. I know you got a cherry Pop because that is your favorite. Am I right?"

Laila was blushing. She was as red as the Popsicle that she held in her hand. She tightened her thighs as she envisioned him between them. His mouth wide and suctioned to all of her glory. "Yeah, you're right. But you are so nasty too. But I like it." Laila smiled as she envisioned the night before.

She and T.C. were celebrating her birthday. She had asked him to plan everything and he did. He had sent her out with her girlfriends to go shopping with his credit card. While she was at the mall he went to her apartment and lavished it with beautiful bouquets of flowers and soft scented candles. He had bought one of the Old School CD's that played the slow jams so that they could get their grind on. He had a bottle of champagne on chill. When he got the signal from one of her girlfriends that she was on her way home he ran her a bath with bubbles that were thick and sensuous. He wanted Laila to have it all and he wanted to be the one to give it to her. He was in love with her in so many ways. He turned out all of the lights so that there was only a glow from the lighted candles. The room was softly scented and he was impressed with his work. He pulled the small package from his pocket and opened it. He smiled down at the two-carat diamond ring that he had bought for her. It was not a wedding ring but a birthstone ring. He knew that she would love it just as he loved her. He put the box back into his pocket and waited to hear her footsteps on the stairs. After what seemed like forever he heard her yell out to her girlfriends, "Thank you'll. I will see you later at the club." T.C. grinned to himself and thought, not tonight you won't. He struggled to keep his penis at ease because it was demanding to stand at attention. It was ready for attack at the mere sound of her voice. T.C. looked down and commanded, "Down boy." Laila put the keys in the door and pushed it opened. She stopped and was speechless because she was halfway startled and the other half surprised and overwhelmed. She dropped the bags that filled her hand and walked slowly over to T.C. Her eyes beginning to fill with tears, she grabbed him by his shirt and pulled him to her. She kissed him gently on his lips and just before breaking down in full tears she blurted out, "I love it! I love you!" She released his shirt and threw her arms around his neck and they kissed hard and continuously.

T.C. pulled the box from his pocket once again and pulled his lips from hers and spoke, "I was going to give this to you later but I can't wait."

He placed his finger under her chin and looked into her eyes and did not speak again until he knew that he had her full attention. He took her hand in his and he placed the box in her palm. Laila's heart was racing. She knew that it was not a wedding ring because they had already discussed those plans but she knew her man and her man would give her nothing but the best. She slowly opened the box and she squealed, "Oh T.C. it is beautiful! I don't know what to say. This is the best birthday that any girl could wish for." She placed the ring on her finger and kissed him deeply again. When they finally came up for air he took her hand and led her to the bedroom. He slowly unbuttoned the six buttons on her blouse. He pulled it away from her shoulders and planted small kisses against her skin. He unzipped her skirt and tugged at it until it moved down her hips and over her thick thighs and fell to the floor. He reached beneath the folds of her blouse to her back and undid the hooks of her bra. He removed both her blouse and her bra and she stood in front of him in her panties and stilettos. He took a step back and admired her. He felt himself growing and once again he restrained. He wanted to take her right there. He wanted to lift her and toss her onto the bed and raise her legs high and wide and put his face all in her wetness. He wanted to enter her deeply and hear the flesh of both of them smacking wickedly together as he fucked her. But tonight he would move slowly. Laila always felt bashful when he looked at her like that. She was not the perfect skinny little petite girl. She had never been skinny and had never desired to be. T.C. stepped back into her space and feeling her self-consciousness he reminded her of how beautiful she was to him. He took her hands and he led her to the bathroom. He placed his hand in the water to see if it was warm because he had filled it with hot water so that it would not be too cold by the time they were ready to get in. It was perfect. As perfect as Laila was to him. He kissed her gently and then he nestled his nose into her neck telling her, "I love the way you smell." He nibbled at her neck. He moved his mouth to her breast and licked each of her nipples. "I love the way you taste." Laila moaned and her nipples hardened. he cupped her breasts and pressing them together he feasted hungrily. Laila ran her fingers across his head pressing him into her breasts. She begged him to suck her nipples, to bite at her swollen mounds. She wanted them to ache. She wanted to feel the pain of their lovemaking. T.C. pulled at one of her nipples with his teeth and she let out a groan. It was pleasure mixed with pain and she loved it. He placed small bites down her belly until he caught the lace removed her stilettos. Her feet once again planted on the floor he kissed the top of them. He bowed over them and he told her, "Your majesty your wish is my command." Laila grabbed both sides of his head and pulling his face up to look at her she said plain and quite simple, "Lick!" T.C. nestled his face in her freshly shaven pubic hair and found his way to her clit where he did as he was told. Laila spread her legs wider. T.C. moved and positioned his body so that he was under her. He pushed his tongue up into her opening and he sucked her as he brought it back out. Laila began moving her body so that she was riding his tongue. She was sweating as if she had been doing hours worth of aerobics. His tongue felt good and thick inside of her. He grabbed her buttocks to steady her and to give her support as he worked her labia and clit. She felt him everywhere. She felt herself tightening and she told him to stop. He stood up and he turned her around as if he were the police and he was about to frisk her. He put one of his legs between hers and pushed them apart and bent her over the tub. He smacked her buttocks with the palm of his hand. He reached around to her front and ran his fingernails against her pubic hair. He slid his finger into her wetness and she moaned. He slid in another finger and she moaned again. He nibbled at her back and in his neck and the other between her legs and she massaged herself with her fingers. They had nothing to hold onto but each other. Laila's mind was all over the place. She felt herself coming and her hand moved quickly and steadily against her clit. T.C.'s breath was harsh and out of control as were his words as he grunted in her ear. She felt the warm liquid squirt between the opening of her thighs and she and T.C. fell back onto the floor. They stayed that way for a few moments before Laila took his penis into her hands. T.C. looked over at the tub and said, "Oh well so much for the bubble bath." Laila was suddenly snapped out of her trip down memory lane. She heard T.C.'s voice calling out to her.

"Hello! Hello earth to Laila!"

"Oh I am so sorry T.C. my mind wandered for a minute."

"A minute? You must have suffered temporary brain freeze from sucking on that Popsicle a little too hard. Damn! That is one lucky Popsicle." T.C. said laughingly.

THE AFFAIR

When you came to tell me
I was not the only one
who had shared your heart
I remember feeling weak
my whole world had
come apart

for years I thought I was
the only one who would
lie upon your chest at one
point I thought you were
joking playing a game,
giving me a test

it was not until I looked
into your eyes that I felt
the pain you had just
shattered my trust my tears
they came like the rain

the one person in my life
I would never have to
suspect how could you
violate our love humiliate
me with your disrespect

all of the nights that I
waited for you praying
that you would make it
safely home you were
lying with someone else
I sat patiently and alone

you even had the audacity
to select someone we
both knew my heart was
savagely raped by not just
one but two

the way the mere thought
of you would shed so
much light now covers
me with darkness
because of thoughts of
you with her at night

what am I to do with all
of this? the images that
plague my mind
I am on my knees praying
to God
To take me even though it
is not my time

I am so angry with you
you did not have the right
to kill my spirit to make
me not want my life

when I look into the
mirror my hair, my eyes,
my skin
I question what was
wrong with me wrong
color, too fat, too thin?

what about our children?
what do you think they see
I am their mother you were
suppose to be loving me
I wonder if they are
blaming me accusing me
of what you've done be a
man and tell them
I am not the villain you
are the one

now you expect
forgiveness for me to
just look the other way
pick up all of the pieces
act as though this did not
happen yesterday

you are even worried
that I might try to even
the score but you have
definitely got it confused
I do not sleep around she
was the whore

now you say that you
are sorry you need a
second chance to make
things work why should
I consider your feelings
when you treated mine
like dirt

we said our vows together
I clearly remember every
word to love and to honor
obviously it is not what
you heard

I have so many mixed
emotions so I need to
scream and yell why did
you do this to me turn my
Heaven into such hell

I wish that I could really
hate you but I have loved
you too hard and too long
my heart is too forgiving
God has taught me that to
hate is wrong

our life will never be the
same again a part of us
has died
I almost wish that you
had not told me that we
had been living a lie

if only I were dreaming
from this deep sleep I
would awake to find that
this nightmare had all
been a huge mistake

you can never imagine
my pain because this has
never been done to you
what goes around comes
around you cannot have
your cake and eat it too

all I can do is pray for
you more than I pray for
myself how ironic that a
weak man would make
me stronger by loving
someone else.

POINT OF INSANITY

The weatherman said that today would be sunny and warm. The rain that was thumping furiously on the pavement outside told me that his forecast must have been for another state. I grabbed the long gray trench coat from the hanger and cursed the rain as I put it on. The oversized umbrella that had sat in the ceramic stand was now opened wide and shielding my newly styled hair. Again I cursed the rain because I had just paid two hundred and fifty dollars for the long wavy locks that softly framed my face. I tried to tiptoe between the raindrops so that my Jimmy Choos would not get wet but that was wishful thinking. If I had not been running late I would have had time to dig out my rain boots that were buried somewhere deep in the back of my overstuffed closet. I could have parked the car in the garage last night but the trashcans had been left once again in front of the door. Now I was cursing my husband David. "That sorry bastard," I grumbled to myself. Hitting the button on my keypad the car door unlocked. I struggled with the umbrella and bumped my head as I was getting into the seat. I shook my head in disbelief and tossed the umbrella to the back onto the floor of the car. I didn't need the complications of the rain not after the night that I had. I didn't want to relive the moment but my mind was being cruel. It was being so very, very cruel. I began to cry. The tears came hard. They were my own personal floods of pain. Why did God give us hearts if He was going to allow them to be broken? I pressed my head against the steering wheel and the horn blasted. That was my wake up call to bring me out of my painful trance. I was already late and I needed to get my ass to work. I started the car and slowly backed it out of the driveway. My neighbors were standing in their doorway. Husband and wife huddled together trying to figure out when it would be a good time to make a dash to their car. He was playfully trying to push her out into the rain and she tenderly smacked his cheek and he gently kissed her on the lips. I paused and watched what once had been my old life. The old life that was now in as much fury as this storm. My neighbors saw that I was looking and they smiled and waved. I lightly tooted the horn but I did not smile back. I was envious and angry at their love. I fumbled with the knobs on the stereo system until I found the Smooth Jazz station. There was always something about jazz that could bring me to a peaceful place and I needed my mind to be at peace and my heart to be still. I rolled my head around and then from side

I smiled at the thought of that and could feel the warmth covering my insides.

"Thanks Jasmine you're the best."

I clicked over to view my missed call and my husband's number appeared.

My first instinct was to press the delete button but instead I pressed the call button. He did not answer right away and just when I was beginning to become annoyed with that hip hop music that he had recorded on his phone he answered. For a moment I just listened to him say hello. His voice was so smooth and sexy. That voice that would send me over the edge every time we made passionate love. He would even speak to me in French sometimes. All he knew though was what was on the label of the French bread that we purchased from our local grocery store. I do not know what the package really said but I would be hot as hell by the time he finished whispering it in my ear. I closed my eyes and I imagined his kiss, his touch and his manhood. Then I remembered that his manhood had been dipping into another flavor.

"Hello Tracy? Tracy are you there?"

I cleared my voice and my thoughts. "Yes I am here. Why don't you change that stupid music on your phone?"

I suddenly remembered how pissed and angry that I was.

"And why are you calling me? I can not imagine what you could possibly have to say."

There was silence for a moment then he spoke, "Tracy we need to talk. Face to face to figure this out. I know that you are hurt and disappointed but we have to discuss this."

I thought to myself, now the motherfucker wants to talk. I did not care if he wanted to talk in sign language, Foreign language, tongue or TTY/TDD. There was nothing and I mean absolutely nothing that he could say. I was tired of his lies.

"Now you want to talk. I was home every night waiting for you so that we could do just that. But where were you? Oh yeah that's right you were in the Land of Oz too busy fucking your secretary Dorothy. No you do not need to talk to me. You need to take your ass back down the yellow brick road and ask her where you can put your clothes. And not the ones I paid for because they will be fueling my fireplace."

There was more silence. I know that he is not tuning me out. There were a few more moments of silence before he spoke.

"Look, do not start that Waiting to Exhale bullshit! Do not fuck with my clothes."

I held the phone away from my face and looked at it. Did I hear him correctly? He steps out on me and he wants to play Mr. Tough guy. That is a hell to the no!

I snapped back at him, "Or what David? What are you going to do? Are you going to tell the wizard? Huh Mr. cowardly lion."

I could hear his fingers tapping his desk then he said sarcastically, "Are you finished being childish? I said that I was sorry. I know that I made an awful mistake. Damn what is it going to take? I am not perfect and never claimed to be. You had some responsibility for what happened too."

Now in my mind I was puzzled because I could not think of a thing that I had done to contribute so I asked him how I was responsible for him putting his dick in between another woman's legs.

And just like all cowards he said, "You were not there for me when I needed you."

I took a deep breath and then I let it fly.

"What in the HELL are you talking about? Where was I David? Perhaps at work, at the school with our children, at home cooking and cleaning or maybe running errands for your mother so that you could catch a plane or two to take your little ho-chick on a romantic escapade. You use that same sorry excuse that every man uses to justify sleeping with another woman. Don't come to me and expect sympathy. You threw everything of value away for a cheap lay. You need to come and get your belongings from the house and preferably while I am not there."

I ended the call and pulled into the space reserved for me, Tracy Masterson. The space next to it was reserved for my husband. I laid my head back against the seat rest and I cursed myself for still loving him.

I wanted to call him back and tell him it was all right but behind my eyes I could see him with her. He was fondling her breasts. His tongue teasing her nipples and then making a trail to her stomach and onto her thighs. I saw him kissing her there. She was calling his name the way I would have called him. I saw him find her erotica and my tears came. She was looking at me and laughing. She was taunting me as he mounted her. She licked her lips and smiled. The tap on the window startled me. I looked through the drops of rain and there she stood with her painted on smile and her big brown eyes. Obviously he had not told her that I knew about their little love affair. She couldn't be that bold to approach me could she? This trick was about to receive a serious ass whipping. Everything was flashing before my eyes. I could hear him telling her how special she was. I wanted to put my hands around her throat and squeeze until all of the anger was out of me. I wanted my peace of mind and my life returned to me. She tapped the window again and I looked so intensely into her eyes that I could see through her skull. My anger was now rage and as I gripped the door handle I could feel the metal pressing into my palm. My heart was beating heavy and hard in my chest. I stood to face her.

LOVE THY NEIGHBOR

I sat on my front porch and watched as the moving men carried in the winter white sofa with its matching pillows tossed onto the top of it. They looked as if they were performing a circus act as they tried to balance the sofa so that the pillows would not drop to the ground. I had to admit that they were rather cute. Especially the one, who had on the tight fitted shirt, he had obviously cut the sleeves off to make them short because they were not the same lengths. I tried to act as if what they were doing were of no interest to me so every once and awhile I would flip through the pages of my magazine so I would not appear to be too nosey. They were just about finished and taking in their last load when one of them yelled from the back of the truck.

"Hey Darius do you want this piece of carpet that you laid on the floor of the truck?"

There was a yell back from the inside of the house, "Naw man, that's trash. Take it to a Dumpster for me." I stood up from my porch swing and stretched. My tank top raised up above my belly button and exposed my flat stomach. I reached for my glass of iced tea and took a long sip. Just as I had finished swallowing I heard a voice say from behind me.

"You have been watching us sweating and working like dogs over here and you didn't even offer us one sip of whatever that is you are drinking."

I turned and looked over my shoulder. His eyes were as bright as his gorgeous smile. I tried to speak but I guess some of the liquid caught in my throat and the only thing that I could get out was a cough.

He chuckled and said, "Don't choke on me now. I haven't had to perform CPR in quite some time."

I coughed a couple of more times and finally getting my voice back I told him, "I wouldn't imagine that they would allow drinking on the job. What if you were to drop and break someone's valuables?"

We both laughed and he extended his hand upward to meet mine.

"Hi, I'm Darius. And just for the record the valuables all belong to me so I am not worried about breaking anything or drinking on the job."

"Nice to meet you Darius and welcome to the neighborhood. Where are you and Mrs. Darius from? Or should I not assume that there is a Mrs.?"

"No, your assumption is correct. Mrs. Harper will be along soon. She would not trust me to handle this all by myself. In fact I better get back to moving things inside before the old ball and chain puts me in the doghouse out back."

We both laughed again. She is one lucky woman I was thinking to myself as I caught myself starring just a tad bit too long at those sexy green eyes and tan muscles. My husband was built and fine too but there was nothing wrong with looking at eye candy just as long as you did not take a piece from the jar. Some things you need to keep a lid on. Damn, now I would have to make sure that I looked fabulous every time that I sat out on my front porch. My last neighbor was over eighty years old and blind.

"Yes you better get back to work. It was very nice to meet you. Tell your wife that I said welcome to the neighborhood and if you . . . I mean if the two of you need anything just give Keith and I a yell."

"We will do that. Can I assume that Keith is your husband? And you are Mrs . . . ?"

"Oh I'm sorry. Yes Keith is my husband and I am Mrs. Perkins. Mrs. Sandra Perkins."

A red Porsche pulls up into the driveway and Darius turns to walk towards it. I could not see the face of the driver but I could see that it was a female so I presumed it was his wife. I waved at him and turned towards my doorway. Just as I had stepped into my house I hear the voice of the female yell out.

"Hey Babe."

I look back and I see his wife step out of the car. She is just as beautiful as he is. I close the door and I mumble "Lucky bitch."

That was two and a half years ago. Since that time Darius and his wife Kathy had become great friends. We spent a lot of time together as couples. If they were not at our house we were at theirs. Both Kathy and my husband Keith had jobs that required them to travel a lot. In fact Darius was just as frustrated as I was that they spent so much time away from home.

But we always tried to keep one another company. If Keith was away Kathy and Darius looked after me and when Kathy was gone Keith and I looked after Darius. But one spring both Kathy and Keith were on travel at the same time and Darius and I ended up on a night on the town together. We decided to try out a new restaurant that was on the other side of town. We ordered dinner and decided to have a little wine, which somehow turned into a lot of wine. We laughed and talked about the usual stuff but then the conversation turned sexual. We began talking about our personal sexual preferences and about what our significant others were like in bed. At first the conversation was pretty general but then Darius ordered a bottle of champagne with strawberries. My head was already fuzzy from the wine but we were having such a great time that I thought what the hell. The waiter opened the champagne and Darius picked up a strawberry and held it to my lips. I took a bite and he said, "That was not sexy at all. I know that you can do better than that." I took it as a dare and when he held another strawberry to my lips I seductively let my tongue slide out of my mouth and touch the tip of the strawberry before biting it. I smiled at him and asked, "Better?" He smiled back at me and winked. We continued eating the strawberries and drinking

"Darius are you sure that you can drive? Maybe we should sit here for a minute. Should I get you some coffee?"

"You can't even walk. How are you going to get me something?"

"I can walk. It was just the high heels that I have on."

He looked down at my feet and he began to laugh. His head fell onto the steering wheel hitting the horn.

"What is so funny, I asked him as I began to laugh along with him."

He lifted his head and looked over at me and then towards the floor of the car and pointed at my feet.

"Where is your other shoe?"

"What do you mean?" I looked down at my feet and sure enough I had lost one of my shoes. I unbuckled my seat belt and started to look around in the front of the car. I leaned over to his side and as I came back up he caught my face and we kissed. Realizing what we were doing we pulled away from one another. We looked at one another and both of our minds were questioning if we really wanted to do this. I knew that it was not right to love thy neighbor but I wanted him. I don't know if it was the alcohol or if it had always been a secret desire. I only knew that I wanted him right then and right now. I leaned in to him and he met me half way. We kissed deep and eagerly. His hands found their way to my breasts that were already firm and ready to be fondled. His kiss was perfect and sloppy all in the same sequence. I could not breathe but I did not want too. I knew that if I caught my breath I would come to my senses. I moved one of his hands to my thigh. I wanted him to touch me. My body was moist and I could feel the dampness of my panties. I kissed him deeper hoping that my urgency would make him devour me. He pulled the straps of my dress down and took one of my breasts into his mouth. His breath mixed with the dampness of my skin felt cool as he sucked and pulled at my harden nipple. I used my hand to push it further into his mouth. I wanted him to be rough with me. He moved his hand further up my thigh and once he found my opening he inserted two fingers. I felt sudden pleasure as I felt his palm brush against my clit. He moved away from my breast and was now nibbling at my neck. I reached across to unbuckle his pants but he stopped me. He whispered in my ear, "Lets go home." He removed his hand from under my dress and started the car. Neither of us spoke as we drove towards the house. We were afraid that we would talk ourselves out of what we were about to do. Darius pulled up into the driveway and we weren't sure whose house to go to. I took out my keys and got out of the car. I opened the front door and Darius followed behind me and closed the door. He grabbed me and turning me around he pressed me against the door. He pulled my dress up to my waist and pulled my panties down. He went down to his knees and grabbing my buttocks he pulled my vagina to his face and he licked my clit with the tip of his tongue. I squealed from the sensation and grabbed the back of his head. I lifted my leg over his shoulder so that he would not have to work hard for his meal. He was no gentleman. His tongue flickered in and out of me. He made sounds that turned me on even more. I was moaning and groaning and begging him to stop and then not to stop. I pushed him away. I reached for the bottom of my dress that was now twisted around my waist and hoisted it over my head. I removed my mangled bra and I stood in front of him naked. I grabbed his hand and pulled him up off of his knees and led him up the stairs to the guestroom. I pushed him back onto the bed and dropped between meeting with him tonight at the restaurant where it had all began. Keith and Kathy were out of town as usual so we would have the entire weekend to indulge in our sexual pleasures. I pulled into the parking lot and before getting out I looked into the mirror to check my hair and lipstick. I went inside and there he was sitting at our table. The waiter brought our usual meal along with the champagne and the strawberries. Darius selected one of the ripe berries from the tray and extended it to me. Just as I leaned forward to take a bite he dropped it. I looked at him and he had a puzzled look on his face. I asked him, "What's wrong babe?" Ignoring me he continued to look straight ahead. I turned and looked over my shoulder to see what had caught his attention. I was speechless when I saw my husband Keith and his wife Kathy sitting on the other side of the restaurant sharing a passionate kiss, champagne and strawberries.

THE BETTER HALF

Olivia brushed the loose strands of hair away from her face and took a closer look at herself in the bathroom mirror. Who was this person that was starring back at her? She did not recognize herself especially after the acts that she had committed the night before. She looked at the images that were behind her in the reflection of the mirror. She could see the crumpled sheets that were lying at the foot of her bed. The pillows that adorned the top of it each day were now thrown about the room as if a tornado had swept through the room. All from her night of restless sleeping. She questioned whether the acts that had been committed would return to haunt her. She turned the faucet on and ran her fingers through the stream of cold water. She cupped her hands together allowing a small pond to form in her palms before splashing it onto her face. She sucked in her breath and let her mind re-encounter the events from the night before. She re-called the tall tan and almost perfect woman that had stood before her. She was beautiful. The type of woman that was and would always be envied. Her name was Sarah and she was long and slender with curves that were in all of the right places. Her shapely legs were enhanced as she stood so graciously in the five-inch stiletto heels that added at least another three inches to her height. I tried hard not to stare at her but her mouth was painted perfectly to match her freshly manicured nails. When she laughed her hair would bounce against her shoulders and then lay gently in the crease of her neckline. I was envious. She was the woman I had always dreamed of being. She had a confidence that I had always wished for but could not quite master. I offered her something to drink in hopes that she would accept because I definitely needed one to take the edge off. The conversation between the two of us was light and entertaining. We shared a lot of common interests and I could see her as being one of my friends but we were just getting to know one another. We were just about to partake in our second glass of wine when the doorbell rang. I excused myself for a moment and when I opened the door there was Paul. He was a very handsome man. Somewhat on the thin side but none-the-less he could hold his own. His small frame did nothing to compare with his enormous ability to perform in the bedroom. We had several rendezvous over the course of three years and each time I was amazed at what he brought to the table. He was very creative and for a man he was very communicative about what he liked and how he pot that was boiling on top of the stove. I re-entered the living room and Paul was now grilling Sarah about some presidential debate. I scolded him because I told him this was my first dinner invitation extended to Sarah and I did not want her to be bombarded with serious conversation, especially after the long day that we both had at the office. Paul stood to remove his suit jacket and loosen his tie. Sarah stood and did the same. I assumed that it was too hot so I went over to the thermostat and adjusted the temperature. I crossed the room and opened the French doors that led out to the balcony. I turned to face both of them and Paul was now removing his trousers and Sarah was on the last button of her blouse. I stood there dumbfounded for a moment and then Paul looking straight into my eyes held out his hand. I did not move. Instead I asked the two of them, "What in the hell is going on?"

Sarah spoke first, "Paul let me in on a little secret that you had a fantasy that you wanted to have fulfilled." Paul cleared his throat and spoke just above a mumble; "Well actually I was the one who had the fantasy. I was just hoping that Olivia would be open-minded and that she would be accommodating."

Now they were both looking at me and waiting for an answer. Did he say accommodating? I needed another drink. No I needed to excuse myself and that is just what I did. I went into the kitchen and opened the oven and wondered if I should take the chicken out or just get into the oven with it. I took the chicken out and placed it on top of the stove next to the pot of cabbage. I stirred the pot and turned the flame off. Everything was hot including Paul and Sarah. I did not know what to do. I did have a fleeting moment of thought about what it would be like with a threesome but my fantasy was with two men and myself. I stood there silently for a moment when Paul entered the kitchen and asked, "Olivia are you all right?"

I felt him starring at my back as he waited for an answer. I was not sure as to what to say so I nodded my head yes. He walked up behind me and put his arms around me.

He whispered in my ear, "I don't want you to do anything that you do not feel comfortable doing but aren't you a least bit curious?"

I felt his hands reach around to unbutton my blouse. I grabbed his hands and gripped them tightly. He stopped and let them fall to my waist.

I spoke softly, "We never discussed this. You never mentioned that you wanted to do this."

He put his arms around me again and kissed my cheek. "Would you have said yes? If your answer is yes, then it should be yes now."

I thought about it for a moment and he was right. If he had asked me I would have said yes. We were both discreet and had ventured in many sexual escapades but they had never included anyone else. We had tried all of the numerous toys and gadgets and positions and gimmicks and had laughed with one another about them. But now there was going to be a third party. Would she be as discreet? I did not know her well at all and I was not sure if that was a good or bad thing. But I did trust Paul and I trusted that he would not invite anyone to join in with us if he did not feel that there would be complete and total indiscretion. Paul reached to unbuttoned my blouse again and this time I did not stop him. He pulled it slowly down and around my shoulders and I felt the fabric tease the hair on my skin. He placed small kisses on my shoulders and then he placed one on the side of my neck. The blouse fell quickly to the floor but in my mind everything was moving in slow motion. His hands cupped my breasts. He kneaded my nipples between his fingers and I felt them become as hard and erect as his penis that was pressing into my buttocks. He pulled at them until he heard me moan. He pressed his manhood harder against me. Placing his hands at the hem of my skirt he raised it up until it was above my buttocks. He moved his hands forward. He placed one hand inside the front of my panties and stroked me gently touching my opening but not venturing inside. I felt his warm breath on my earlobe as his breathing became harder. I began to move my body with the rhythm of his finger. I moaned again and Sarah walked in asking, "Is everything okay in here?" I jumped and tugged to pull my skirt down and to cover my breasts. Paul turned me around to face Sarah. He reached around and unbuttoned my skirt and pulled it to the floor. He then pulled down my panties until they were around my ankles and when I did not move my feet so that he could remove them he lifted them himself. He then removed my arms from my breasts and licked my nipples. I heard Sarah respond; "I guess so." Paul now had a mouthful of my breast and was enjoying it quite thoroughly when Sarah who was naked down to her panties walked over and began to devour the unattended one. There was so much sucking and licking going on that I felt left out. I placed my hand on Sarah's breast and they were perfected in size and they were truly hers. Her skin was soft and smooth. I fondled her nipple that had already become erect. I placed it into my mouth and swirled my tongue over it. I suckled it while she and Paul took turns suckling mine. Paul covered my mouth with his and he kissed me deeply. I felt his tongue dancing in my mouth and then I felt a tongue between my thighs teasing at my opening. I tried to break away from Paul but he had me pinned against the counter. I felt the tongue ease in and out of my opening. The small kisses that came in between each stroke as her tongue slid down and across my clitoris. Paul's hands were now rough and greedily stroking my breast. My hands were idle. I reached down and grabbed his penis. It was hard and I felt his veins protruding as if they about to burst. He nibbled at my neck and this made me stroke him more aggressively. He grabbed Sarah by her hair and pulled her up. No I thought to myself. I did not want her to stop. But it did not stop because he took her place. But he was not as gentle. He savagely went to town on my vagina and it felt as if I was going to lose

Today was her daughter Tamara's high school graduation and she could not have felt more proud. She wanted the day to be perfect for not only her daughter but for herself as well. They both had been through a lot of struggle since the divorce. No matter what the age a child will always feel the loss when a parent moves out of the home. Today was a special day and Samantha was going to make an extra special effort to tolerate her ex-husbands' often too critical comments about her. She had lost a considerable amount of weight since the divorce partly from stress but mostly from the vigorous workout she got after joining a gym. She cut her hair and that actually made her look ten years younger. She had always taken care of herself but it had been for everyone else' benefit. This time around she was looking out for herself and doing things the way she liked. In fact she was going to have highlights put in her hair today and she even thought about having a couple more inches cut off. She thumbed through the magazine not really focusing on any of the articles because her mind just would not keep still. All she could concentrate on was seeing her daughter walk across the stage and receive her diploma. It had been a long journey for her daughter because after her father left the house she felt abandoned. She did not speak to him for a long time and she distanced herself from family and friends. It had taken months of therapy to get her to focus on school and other social activities. Tears welled up in Samantha's eyes as she thought about all of the pain that her child had endured. As her mother she had dealt with her own guilt of not protecting her from that pain. But then again how could she when she could not protect herself from the devastation of the divorce? She shook her head and her shoulders because today was not the day to dwell on this. She was determined to be in good spirits and to make this one of the happiest days in her daughter's life. The dryer clicked off and Samantha pushed the hood away from her head. She undid one of the curlers to feel if her hair was dry. Monica, her stylist motioned for her to come over and sit in her styling chair. Monica was always filled with gossip that Samantha was always eager to hear. She did not watch the soap operas on television but she loved the hell out of Monica's sagas. By the time she had left the salon she knew who was cheating, dying, in jail, and pregnant. Samantha headed out of the door of the salon and headed towards her parked car when she heard someone calling her name. The voice sounded familiar. She turned and looked across the parking lot and she saw her ex-husband's new wife. Samantha you walking to your car. I ran because I didn't think that you saw me"

Samantha looked at her and said, "And?"

Amber smiled that typical I am clueless smile and continued. "And I thought that we could have lunch?' Samantha stood silently for the moment. Her lips did not move but her mind said, Hell to the capital No!

Samantha cleared her throat and said, "Amber, as you know Tamara is graduating this evening. When would there be time to have lunch? I have a million things left to do and because you insisted on having the party at your house I can only assume that you do not have any spare time either."

Amber gave her a smile and one of those are-you-kidding—me glances.

"Oh come on Samantha there is plenty of time and besides everything is being catered there is really nothing to do. We all have to eat. Besides I want to tell you all about the magnificent gift that James and I got for Tamara."

Samantha could have cared less. She just wanted to be on the other side of town and not standing in front of this nut case but she knew that Amber would continue her whining so she gave in. She hit the entry button on her car keys to re-lock her car and followed Amber. Amber flicked her hair back away from her shoulder and as she did Samantha mimicked her. She could not help but smile to herself as she thought about how Amber represented all of the women whom had no butt. Then she laughed out loud when the thought hit her that she had always thought that her husband James was an ass man. This was apparently not so. Obviously it must have been what she was allowing him to do between the cheeks that had turned him on. Amber turned and looked over her shoulder at Samantha with a puzzled look on her face. Samantha just smiled and waved her hand. Once inside of the sub shop they ordered their food and found their way to a small booth in the back. Amber wiggled in her seat and adjusted herself before speaking.

"Well Samantha, as you know Tamara has been hinting around to James for a car and . . ."

Before she could finish Samantha cut in, "Do not tell me that James purchased her a car. I told him not to do that until she had finished her first year. We had agreed on it."

Amber sat back against the cushioned seat. Her brows frowned in towards the center of her head, "I do not know what you and James agreed upon but I know that I shelled out Twenty-eight thousand dollars yesterday down at the dealership."

Samantha leaned forward as if she had not heard correctly what Amber had said and she repeated, "Twenty-eight thousand dollars?" Has James lost his fucking mind she just turned eighteen. What the hell is he thinking? And why in the hell would you do that?"

Amber cleared her throat and becoming just a tad bit annoyed replied, "Because he is my husband and if he wants the best for Tamara so do I. Don't you think that she deserves it? She is a good kid." She sat back in her seat feeling confident that she had given a satisfactory answer.

Samantha let out a loud sigh and said, "Key word here is kid. If you wanted to buy her a car why not get something small and affordable. Let her have some responsibility. I did not raise her to believe that everything was going to be handed to her."

Amber decided to play with fire and she said, "Well James and I have the money and we want her to have it."

Samantha leaned in real close across the table and without stuttering she told Amber, "You may have money Amber but James does not have a pot to piss in. Now just because you want to be his sugar mama does not mean that you are going to set that example for my child. I suggest you return the car and get your money back or drive the damn thing yourself because Tamara is my child and I am telling you that she is not going to take it."

Amber flung her hair back and leaned in towards Samantha and matching the tone in Samantha's voice she said, "She is James's daughter too!"

Samantha leaned back in her seat and folded her arms, "Is she?"

Amber gasped and stood up from the table, "I can not believe that you just said that to me. You are still jealous that James left you for me. Well with remarks like that I can see why."

Samantha stood and looking Amber straight in her eyes she told her, "Mad as hell yes, but jealous no. Once you learn that you have shit you don't want to keep it. So I got smart and moved on. I've learned to not let a man use me."

Amber put her hands on her hips, "And so you are saying that James is using me?"

Samantha stepped away from the table and put her purse on her shoulder. She walked past Amber stopping to whisper in her ear, "See you later Sugar mama."

She turned and left the restaurant. As she walked hurriedly to her car she felt the tears begin to well up in her eyes. Amber's words were true. She was jealous and she hated the feeling. She wanted the best for her daughter but she wanted to be the one to give it to her. She knew that James had only left her for Amber's money and lifestyle. She reminded herself that nothing was supposed to ruin the day but once she was inside of her car behind the tinted windows she cried. Samantha headed home with a heavy heart. She had dreamed of this day. The day that she and James would watch their daughter take her first steps into adulthood. Nowhere in her dream did she find another woman. She had only been with Amber for an hour and it seemed that she had sucked the life out of her. She hated that bitch. Everything that she and James had shared he was now sharing with the other woman. The other woman being Amber. Samantha made it home and the only thing she wanted to do was to get a stiff drink but there was not anytime for that. Instead she filled the tub with warm water and added scented bath oil beads and tried to forget the incident of the day. Just as she was beginning to doze off her phone rang. She glanced down at the cell phone on the floor and the incoming call was from James. Just great, just freaking fantastic Samantha thought. She assumed that he was calling to throw around a few obscenities because she knew that Amber had went home whining like the little bitch that she was. She pushed the talk button and placed the phone on speaker and answered coyly, "Yes James, and before you start with the shit let me tell you that I am not in the mood."

James laughed and asked her, "What are you mumbling about? I need to know if you still have those folding chairs in the garage? We may need a few extra ones to put out on the patio deck. If you can bring them when you come . . ." He paused to wait for her response.

When she did not give one he continued. ". . . Or if it is an inconvenience I can come and pick them up."

Samantha sucked her teeth, "Why would you come all the way out here if I am coming there? That's a no brainier isn't it?"

James replied, "You never know with you. I am damn if I don't and more damn when I do. Thanks and I will see you when you get here."

Samantha pushed the end button and stretched out again in the tub. James voice brought back memories. She thought of their first night together. Instead of going out she decided to cook for him. He was very surprised not because of the cooking but because she wore a maids outfit while she did it. She remembered how he stood behind her when she bent over to check on the roasted chicken and she felt his hands on her buttocks. The way he squeezed them with just the right amount of pressure. And somehow the butter ended up on her breast instead of the dinner rolls. Her insides tingled as she visualized his fingers tugging at her thong as he pressed her against the cool refrigerator door. She could feel his breath on the side of her neck as she waited for him to kiss her there. She felt his knee press her thighs open wider as he found her spot. She remembered how he teased her after they had sex because he had found her G-spot. He told her that he had put an X on it. He was not lying because he could hit it every time. Samantha squirmed in the tub. She was craving James' manhood to be inside of her. She touched herself as she imagined his thickness easing in and out of her. Damn she wished that she had brought her dildo into the bathroom with her. Her finger found her clit and she made soft gentle strokes. She felt the water make little waves against her opening as she slid her buttocks against the bottom of the tub. She wanted James to be there with her. She was throbbing on the inside. She wanted to feel his tongue teasing her. She was wet. Too wet to be alone. She slid two fingers of her one hand inside of her as she stroked her clit with the finger of the other. The water between her legs gushed against her like waves as she made herself orgasm. She cried out Oh God

James! Oh! Oh! Ahhh! She arched her back and then the water became still. She relaxed her body and let the water out of the tub. She suddenly felt cheap and cheated. She ran the shower and stood under the water and as she lathered her body she tried to wash James away. Samantha dressed and went to the garage to get the extra chairs that she promised to bring and headed to the graduation ceremony. Tamara had already left earlier that day to be with her classmates. By the time Samantha arrived James and Amber were already there and seated. She really did not want to sit with them but James motioned that he had saved her a seat. It blew her mind that he had the audacity to sit there in the middle of two women with his chest stuck out. You would have thought that he was going to win a prize or something. They finally called Tamara's name and everyone stood and cheered and the sense of pride was overflowing. Samantha was crying and James offered a hug but she declined. It was obvious that Amber had not mentioned to him what she had said earlier. After all of the graduation hoopla everyone went to James and Amber's house. The party was in full swing and in fact it was close to two in the morning by now. Tamara had left again with her friends and the adults were now doing the old school jams. After about an hour or so things started to wind down and the guests began

James stepped closer to her face, "And if she's not what are you going to do about it?"

He pushed the button and the garage door began to close. He pressed against Samantha and pinned her against the trunk. She pushed at his chest but when he did not step back she knew that he was not joking and that he wanted to fuck her. She stared at him until he kissed her. He kissed her like the first time they made love. He was all over her and she knew that she should say no but she wouldn't. Instead she pulled the thin straps down over her shoulders and pushed her dress to the garage floor. He grabbed her now erect breasts and he licked her nipples. She felt his hands moving down and around her buttocks. In her mind she was telling him that she did not want the foreplay. She just wanted him to enter her. To fuck her because she knew that this opportunity would probably never come again. He lifted her onto the top of the trunk and pushed her legs apart. He wrapped his lips around her clit and she moaned. He stuck his tongue inside of her and she grabbed the back of his head. She moaned his name quietly but she wanted to shout because it felt so good. He came up for air and pushed her back until she rested on her elbows. He placed his hands under her knees and pulled her close enough to enter her. She felt the tip of his penis and she had to hold back from exploding. It still felt good. Just as she had remembered he was thick and hard. Each time he entered her he would go a little further. She looked at him and he looked at her and she told him, "Fuck me James!" And that is exactly what he did. His arms were under her thighs and her legs were extended into the air. He made every thrust count. The sound of her buttocks bumping against the top of the trunk turned her on more. His face tight as he moaned a deep grunting sound and she felt him releasing inside of her. It felt so good that Samantha grabbed her breasts as if she were holding onto her orgasm. James stepped back and pulled up his pants that were down around his ankles. Samantha surveyed her trunk for incriminating damage and found her dress. James was out of breath but he managed to say to Samantha, "Damn girl, you still got it."

In return she replied, "Well so have you. I guess Ex marked the spot literally this time."

When she bent over to pick up her panties James slapped her on her buttocks. Samantha smiled as she entertained the thought that perhaps there would be more opportunities.

fingers ponder in and around her opening and Erique cheered her on. He loved to watch as she explored herself. He wanted to do ten different things to her at once. He placed his mouth at her opening and he sucked her until she felt his teeth pinch the tip of her clitoris. The pain made her flinch and she grabbed his head pulling gently back on it so that he would ease up a little. Erique was a hungry man and he wanted a hungry mans' meal. He raised her up onto the desk and as the papers and pens fell to the floor he ignored them. He pulled his swivel chair up and under him and he leaned forward and pulled her legs over his shoulder. He pushed his tongue into her and she fell back onto the desk and more items fell to the floor. Her knees fell outward and she opened them as far as she could so that he could taste all of her. She wanted his tongue deep inside of her. She loved the way he ate her, the way he licked and teased her. He pulled out of her and making his tongue full he licked her from the top of her vagina to the bottom as if he were licking his plate clean. Lisa's legs began to tremble and she knew that if he did not stop that she would have an orgasm. Erique was not ready for that. He still had quite the appetite. He pushed the chair back and pulled her up and turned her so that she was now hovering over the desk with her buttocks against his penis. He gripped her around her wrists and he bit at her shoulders and back. He was like a kid in a candy store and he just did not know which treat he liked the best. He wanted to lick her, he wanted to fuck her from the rear, pound her from the front, he was greedy and Lisa loved the hell out of it. She did not care how he did it as long as he made her feel good. His hands released her wrists and he bent down and nibbled her butt cheeks. He dug his fingers into her skin and then he smacked them hard. Lisa welcomed the pleasure of her pain. He spanked her again and without warning he entered her. He placed his hands on each side of her hips and raised her buttocks slightly upwards until he was in a good position. She felt his thickness slide up into her valley and around the bend and as he hit that curve she matched his rhythm. Her breasts were moving violently along with the rocking of the desk as he pushed further into her. Lisa was calling out for him to fuck her harder. The nipples of her breasts were firm and they brushed against the desk making them tingle. She released one hand and she massaged them but only for a minute because she felt the desk move forward as Erique's thrust became more forceful. His sweat was now dripping onto her back and she felt it rolling down into the crevices of her behind. Once again she felt herself coming to

Erique looked up to find Lisa his boss, trying to get his attention. He pulled his chair closer to his desk.

"Erique you are covered in perspiration. Are you feeling well?"

Erique cleared his throat and picked up the manila envelope from his desk and handed it to Lisa.

"Yes I am fine Lisa."

His abrupt attitude caught her off guard and left her with suspicion making him soften his tone.

"Its' just a bit warm in here."

Lisa looked at Erique not sure that she quite believed him. "Maybe you should open the window a little."

She stood waiting for him to move towards the window but Erique only nodded in agreement and leaned forward on his desk. His erection was about to spill into his pants and he gritted his teeth to hold back the deep growl that wanted to be released from the back of his throat. After a few moments more of idle conversation Lisa finally turned towards the door. Enrique's leg shook violently as he watched her rounded ass walking away. The door closed and Erique leaned back and let his growl surface and as he felt his volcano erupt he thought of how she had made him cum all in his mind.

SUNDAY BRUNCH

I took a long sip from my glass of champagne and orange juice and hit the button on the remote for the stereo. Oh yeah the smooth sexy sounds of Maxwell floated above my head. I opened the French doors that led outside to the pool deck. The water from the fountain made the water in the pool resemble waves in the ocean. The sun was absolutely gorgeous overhead. The day and my life could not have been more perfect. I was beginning to feel a little guilty about the sexcapade I had with my friend a week ago. Guilty as hell but it was so delicious. I did not know that sin could feel so damn good. They say that revenge is sweet but I beg to differ. Revenge is coming and coming and coming again. I was not being nasty just a little naughty. I could not label myself freak of the week. At least not yet, I couldn't. But I did have every intention of experiencing it all. Finally I was smart enough to be in control. Instead of crying, sulking and focusing on the man who left me and made me feel worthless I was going to focus on living again. I stopped investing my money on buying 'my baby done left me' CD's at Wal-Mart and instead I spent it on top dollar clothing and lingerie. For every pair of

Stiletto's that I owned whether they were lace ups, zip downs, ankle wrapped, snapped and or buttoned, peep toe or pumped I had the outfits to compliment them. After twenty-five years of marriage I was a little out of the game but once you get the ball back things start to come back to you. The sun felt so soothing on my skin. My tan was on point and it made the two-piece bikini that I was sporting look stunning. Of course the red six-inch stilettos that I was wearing were the icing on the cake. Just looking at them made me feel hot and want to be bothered. I walked over to the table that was on the other side of the pool deck and spread the white linen cloth on top of it. I had about thirty minutes to set up for the brunch that I was having at one o'clock. I went back into the house and the doorbell rang. I went to the door and there he stood my eye candy. He was earlier than I had hoped but he was too damn fine for me to be angry. He was in a business suit and looking professional and overdressed for my affair. I took his hand and led him inside.

I kissed him gently, and then said, "You are early."

He poked at his tie and told me that his conference had ended earlier than he had anticipated and rather than go all the way back to his condo he thought he would take the chance and come a little early. I noticed that he was trying hard not to stare at me in my skimpy bikini but the sweat that was forming on his brow told me that he liked what he saw. I rescued him by saying, "I was just about to put the food on the table, you can help if you like. I hope that you are hungry."

He looked at my body and gave me the sinfulness grin then he removed his jacket and tie and handed them both to me. I dropped them to the floor.

He said, "Hey what's up with th . . . ."

Before he could finish his sentence I pushed my body into his and planted a wet kiss on him. Once his hands touched my flesh he was a lost soul. I took his hand and put it on his belt buckle and told him to get undressed.

He looked at me and said, "I didn't bring any trunks with me."

I picked up a fresh strawberry from the tray on the counter and put it into my mouth.

"Oh? Well I do not want you to feel uncomfortable about that."

I reached behind my back and untied the string to my bikini top and tossed it to the floor with his clothes. He smiled and said, "Now I feel better."

I picked up the tray of strawberries and told him to follow me out to the pool. I placed the tray at the edge of the pool. He was standing close enough that when I bent over I could feel his penis on my behind. I stood up and walked to the steps that led down into the pool. Yes stilettos and all. Now I know that sounds crazy but I wasn't worried. This brother was so turned on by this that I knew that I was about to be laid and paid. He dropped his trousers and briefs in one smooth motion and followed me into the pool. He put his hands on my waist and pushed me up against the pool wall. I kissed him and pushed him back. I swam over to the fountain and let the water splash all over my body. I ran my fingers through my hair and then over my breasts. He swam over to me and his hands went up to my hips and in a one, two three motion my bottoms were off. He brought his hands to my breasts and cupped them. He squeezed and fondled them making the water from the fountain flow between them. He suckled and licked each nipple until I moaned for him to stop. He moved my body against the wall and lifted my legs. I watched him go under the water and then the pleasure came. The pressure from the water above and below mixed with his tongue going in and out of my vagina was breathtaking. He licked and sucked my clit until I almost drowned him. He came up and suckled my breasts again while he gently slid his penis between my legs. Each thrust made the water push against my body. It felt so damn good. This was the best water aerobics a girl could ask for. I felt myself coming to an orgasm and I grabbed his buttocks as he grabbed mines. I saw my stilettos rise in and out of the water with each pleasurable thrust. I pushed him deeper and deeper into me as the water splashed savagely around us. The water calmed and we untangled ourselves. He hoisted himself up onto the edge of the pool and I positioned myself in between his legs after all it was Sunday brunch and I had not eaten yet.

was so polite. I watched how he pulled the chair out for the young woman he was with. How he spoke to the waitress. He was very attentive to women. I liked that. I want a man who is going to give me his time. I watched Bill for awhile and when he got up to go to the men's room I decided it was time to go to the ladies room. I waited for him to come out and when he did I casually commented on his tie. I simply said, "Wow that is a nice tie that you have on. It really looks great with that shirt." He smiled and before he could say thank you I added, "I bet your girlfriend gave it to you." He laughed and tugging at the knot he replied, "No, I do not have a girlfriend and I think that I am capable of picking out my own attire." We exchanged names and numbers and we were an item for about three weeks. It was a hot three weeks. One of them we spent on a beach in the Dominican. It was absolutely fantastic. We were on an exclusive beach filled with palm trees and white sand and water for miles. I was lying on my stomach when I felt Bill's hands massaging my shoulders. He picked up the bottle of tanning lotion and poured some in the palms of his hands and then began to spread it evenly all over my body. He cupped my bare buttocks and he kneaded my round mounds in his hands. He slapped them playfully and then he bit each one gently before slowly rolling me over onto my back. Starting with my right inner thigh he kissed it. Then he did the same with my left one. He poured more tanning lotion into his hands and this time cupping my breast he kneaded them squeezing them until I became aroused and my nipples hardened. I spread my legs farther apart and he placed tiny little kisses from the center of my breast down until he found the center of my world. He flicked his tongue teasing my clit and I squirmed. The heat and the mist of the water from the ocean were a true aphrodisiac and I was getting hotter than hell. He opened his mouth and placed it directly over my clit and he suckled it. He mixed pain and pleasure together stopping only to lick it at intervals. I was trying to squeeze my thighs together to hold him in one place but he placed his arms around them and opening them wider he licked and he licked and he licked. I could not move. All I could do was try to endure the pleasure. He kept teasing me to the point that I was like a mad woman. I kept calling out his name begging him for fear that I could not take anymore. But I wanted more. It felt so damn good. I felt his tongue enter me. I was so wet. I wanted him to enter me with his hard penis. I wanted to feel his thickness between my legs. I begged but he continued to hold me down and I felt myself climaxing. My back were wrong. He said no but I could tell that he was lying because he had a strange look on his face. After he glanced at my legs for the fourth time I asked him outright.

"All right is there something wrong with my legs?"

He paused and then he said, "Well, actually I was wondering if you always wore your dresses so short?" Now I had to pause. My dress was too short? What in the hell was wrong with this brother? This was a guy who back in the day would chase anything in a dress regardless of its length. I took a deep breath before I spoke, "I do not think that my dress is too short however if you felt that way I wish that you had mentioned it to me before we left my house. I would have put on something else not that I feel that I need too but I would not have wanted you to feel uncomfortable."

He looked at me and then turning back to look at the road he said, "Well if you advertise someone will eventually answer the add."

What in the hell was he talking about? I could not believe that this man-whore was sitting here judging me as if he had the right. Here I was thinking that I was going to get the fuck of my life but instead I was getting a lecture from Mr. Holy-Roily. I did not need this shit and I was just about to tell him to turn around when he placed his hand on my thigh. I was totally surprised and for a minute I thought about removing it but I did not. I wanted to toy with him a little bit. I wanted to see and feel just how good Mr. Goodie two shoes really was. I slid my body down a little more in the seat and I spread my legs a little farther apart so that he could have easy access. I looked at him waiting for him to frown but he did not. He did however move his hand further up my thigh until he felt the tip of my lace panties. I licked my lower lip and with one of his fingers he pulled my panties to the side and inserted his ring finger into my vagina. Even though he made no comment I could tell that he was aroused by my moistness. He began to slide his finger in and out slowly and upward to massage my clit. I put my hands on the side of my dress and hiked it up further until it was almost around my waist. He continued to massage me and as he became more aroused his language became more sexually verbal. Finally, he seemed as if he were loosening up a little and letting go.

He looked at me and he said, "Damn baby you are so wet."

I did not respond. I wanted to make him work hard. He suggested that we skip dinner and go to his place. I was not going to have him short change me like that. I was all dressed up and I was going to dinner. I moved his hand away and pulled my dress down. A moment ago he was chastising me about advertising. Now he just wanted to lay me down and keep it moving? No I don't think so. I did not roll like that.

"No we are going to dinner," I said firmly.

He seemed a little put off and I just ignored his attitude. I did get to have my six-course meal and it was quite delicious. When we got back to the car I thanked him with a kiss. My lips on his lips and my hand on his penis I was ready to give him his dessert. He pushed my hand away and looked around as if he were afraid that someone had seen us. Now I was really pissed off. What was going on? This could not be the same guy who would drag girls into the locker room and bathrooms and have his way with them. There was no way that he could have changed that much. I backed away from him and I looked directly in his eyes. With my hands on my hips I asked him, "What the hell is your problem?" Don't look at me as if you don't have any idea what I am talking about. I know that you are not a shy guy. Back in the day you would have hit this two or three times by now. So what is the deal?" He let out a huff and he said, "We are in a lighted parking lot or haven't you noticed? We are not in high school anymore you know." It was time to go. He had killed my buzz and frankly I had become bored. I guess he was reading my mind because he held the car door open and motioned for me to get inside. Believe me it was my pleasure. Well it should have been. When we arrived to my house I did not even wait for him to get out of the car. I simply told him thanks for dinner and goodnight. I do not know what had happened to him over the years but he was just too cautious for me. I was really having a dry spell. It had been almost three months and I had not had a good lay in the hay. That weekend my girlfriends and I decided to *cruise'* the clubs and see if there was anything new and different on the scene. After about the third club I was ready to call it a night. They convinced me to go to one more, which was a jazz club. Actually it was not too bad. The atmosphere was calming and after the last two noisy hip-hop havens we had just left this was a welcomed change.

I like hip-hop but I was just not in the mood for the playa-playa vibe. I kicked my stilettos off under the table and stretched my toes. The waiter came and I ordered two Mojitos. I figured the night was another dead end and I may as well get my drink on. I was enjoying the band when I noticed two gentlemen across the room. They would look at me and then turn and engage in conversation. They must be sizing me up. I nodded towards them and they in turn did the same. They were both attractive and that in itself was a warning sign. What should I think two pretty men together? Things that make you go Hmmm. On the other hand maybe this was my lucky night. Could I be in for a double-header? I smiled to myself. Just as a nasty thought was entering my head one of them was approaching me. Oh-oh batters up.

"Excuse me," the fine tall dark chocolate specimen said.

I looked up at him and responded with, "Yes."

"My friend and I were wondering if we could join you, ladies?"

I looked to my girls for signs of disapproval and there were none so I gestured with my hand.

"By all means please do."

He motioned for his friend to join us and we all sat and talked and after awhile I knew which one I was going to be playing the game with. I knew whom I was going to knock out of the park. I felt that I needed to go to the ladies room to freshen up so I excused myself. After finishing in the restroom I opened the door and there he was the fine dark chocolate specimen coming out of the men's room. It was game time. Our eyes met and we both knew what the deal was. The only question was 'your bathroom or mine?' I was too hot and horny to toss a coin so I grabbed his hand and led him into the ladies room. I locked the latch and he locked his lips on me. Oh God I had not been kissed that badly since elementary school. I tried to focus my mind elsewhere but this guy had a tongue like a cow. I broke away and tried to turn my face to the side just as his thick tongue landed on my cheek. Damn it! I was throbbing between my thighs and now my head. I tried to think fast about what I should do. I did not want him to kiss me again so I just tilted my head downward and unbuckled his belt. And wouldn't you know it the brother was packing. I inserted his ding-dong and pushed my forehead into his chest to avoid being kissed again. I was so horny that I knew that I would come quickly. To my surprise I did not. He was long and hard and he moved his penis in and out of me with such magnificent rhythm. It would be just my luck to find a man who could screw me like velvet and kiss like sandpaper. My leg was thrown over his arm and I noticed his biceps as he pressed against the wall to maintain his balance. His upper body was beautiful and that turned me on even more. I was already wet but the moister I became the deeper I wanted him to go. I grabbed his buttocks and urged him to thrust harder. I moaned as I felt his thickness throbbing inside of my vaginal walls. He felt so good. I felt my orgasm coming and I shouted to him, "Fuck me!" I moved my hand to my clit and stroked myself with the same rhythm of his penis. My mouth opened and I knew something wanted to come out but I was speechless. My body tightened and I felt the muscles between my thighs grab his penis as they spasm. There was a knock at the door and I tried to say, "Just a minute," but I could barely get a word out. I wanted to go another round but the spell was broken when he tried to kiss me again. I gave him a quick peck on the lips and I tidied myself up. I unlocked the door and giving him an, I'll call you motion with my hand I hurried back to the table. I never did see that chocolate specimen again. What was the point? I had

SUMMERTIME

The breeze swept silently through the screen of the window making the sheer white curtains dance. The sounds of the saxophone coming from the radio surrounded the room creating the ambience for a thunderous night that would end into a quiet storm. He sat watching as I lathered myself in scented oils. My hands massaging my body awakening my senses as they brought his to arousal. The summer night was filled with the aroma of jasmine, honeysuckle, musk and passion. The ninety-five degree heat was accentuating the aromas as well as the raging hormones that were no longer lying dormant. The sheer curtains blew about him seductively covering his face as though they were playing a game of peek-a-boo. He moaned as I pleasured myself in preparation to please him. He motioned for me to come to him but I naughtily disobeyed. Turning my back to him I bent my body over and let my hands slide slowly down the back of my legs until they reached the heels of my five-inch stilettos. I heard him moan and I smiled in anticipation of the inhibitions that were about to be released. He came towards me crawling on his hands and knees. He positioned himself beneath my pleasure and he tasted me. I moaned and he moaned. Pulling the sheets from the bed to the floor they crumpled around us resembling mounds of beach white sand. I eased my body onto the mound and he placed gentle kisses on the insides of my thighs until he found my seashell. Opening it wide he inserted his tongue and played my body as sultry as the saxophone that could be heard in the distance. I was now as wet as the ocean. My soft subtle skin felt the chill of the light breeze that fondled the nipples of my ample breasts heightening my eroticism. I arched my back and grabbed the blackness of his buttocks as he entered me. I watched the curtains as they danced along with their own rhythm as he rode into the waves of my sexuality. I watched their movement as if I was hypnotized. In and out, in and out my body moving with his in and out, in and out. The breeze stopped and the curtains fell against the wall. I screamed his name as I climbed the wall. He was motionless until he saw Olivia come from behind the trio-folded screen. He was puzzled and his face was filled with question and curiosity. He did not know whether to be angry or turned on by the fact that she had witnessed our sexual encounter. Olivia was definitely turned on and she was ready to show how much she was. She glided across the room her body perfect and moist. She stood in front of me and then kissed me on the lips and almost in a whisper she said, "I hope you saved me some." I wickedly smiled and she turned to join him on the bed where he was now sitting with a look of bewilderment. Taking his hand she led him over to the chair and gently pushed him down to sit. She slowly and seductively pulled the strapless dress above her head exposing her nakedness in front of him. He was in awe and then I saw the guilt come to his face. He looked at me for approval and I smiled and nodded that it was okay. She was a beautiful bronze woman that had a body that any man would want to explore. Even women, myself included, but I had always resisted such taboo until now. Olivia motioned for me to come and I followed her instructions. She moved behind me and placed small kisses on my shoulders and back while she fondled my breasts. Her hands moved down my stomach and then my thighs. She pressed her body into my behind and pushed and moved me until we were in a unison grind. He repositioned himself in the chair as if he were waiting for a good show to begin. I closed my eyes and Olivia placed her hands on my vagina. She quickly inserted two fingers into my opening and I slid my body down until I straddled them. She placed a finger of her other hand on my clit and began stroking it. I moaned and

SPECIAL DELIVERY

The phone rang bringing me out of a sound sleep. I ran my fingers through my hair and randomly looked around the room for the cordless. After about fifteen seconds I realized it was not the phone it was the stupid doorbell. That must have been one hell of a drink that I had at the party last night. I finally made my way to the door and after hearing the furious knocking on the other side of it I was not very gracious.

"Hold your damn horses for Peat's sake."

I swung open the door ready to hurl a few more obscenities when I saw the mailman. He was not the usual guy that had been coming and I was thankful for that. This brother was F.I.N.E. Talk about something that would melt in your mouth. Getting over my speechlessness I said, "Oh my bad. I apologize I thought you were someone else." He did not acknowledge my apology so right away I became defensive. But on the same token I was thinking to myself that I would love to take the wrapping off of this lollipop. I licked my lower lip. He was looking at me as if I was a nut case.

He cleared his throat and said, "I have a package delivery for Janice McKane."

I smiled, "That would be me. The one and only."

He shoved the package in my direction and motioned with the pen in his hand for me to sign the invoice. What was up with this guy? He could have at least smiled at that comment. So I went in for the kill.

"Is it me or are you having a bad day?"

He looked me in the eye and said, "No I am not having a bad day. I am just trying to deliver this package to a woman named Janice McKane. I did not expect to find a beautiful black woman with attitude and a fine ass body dressed in a red lace panty. You have a great day Mrs. McKane."

I was frozen for a moment and then I slowly looked down at myself. I had gone to the door in a fitted tank top and red lace panties. Again I thought to myself, "What in the hell was in that drink?"

Just as he was about to pull away I yelled across the lawn, "Its' Ms."

He pulled away and didn't look back. I closed the door and went into the den. I flicked on the television and plopped myself down on the brown leather sofa. I opened the package and went into frenzy. I had ordered a special dress for the company's Christmas Eve party and this was not it. The party was a week away and that meant there was not anytime for making mistakes. I picked up the phone and dialed the customer service number. After waiting for twenty long minutes and listening to that awful elevator music I finally heard a human voice.

"This is 'Tre-Chique', how can I assist you?"

Taking the attitude that was in my voice out I replied, "I ordered a red chiffon halter dress in a size six and today I received a blue taffeta something or another in a size ten."

The customer service Rep replied, "Ma'am I am so sorry. We can send you the correct order as soon as possible."

I heard the sound of her fingers typing on the keys.

"Your dress will arrive to you in seven to ten business days."

I sucked in my breath and said, "WHAT! This is not acceptable. I need this dress by Thursday of this week at the latest. I heard more typing and then a cough and then more typing.

She finally responded, "We can send it express but we can not guarantee delivery by Thursday. Friday morning would be the latest. Would you like for me to put this through?"

I let out a sigh and told her to process the order. I hung up the phone and kicked the ottoman that was sitting in front of the sofa. I then looked up and saw my reflection in the mirror.

"I need to go and put some clothes on."

I went up to the second level of my townhouse and into the bathroom. I turned on the faucets in the tub and poured in a few baths oil beads. Butt naked and beautiful I slowly entered into the warm and soothing water. I put my head back on the bath pillow and let the rippling from the jet streams take me away. I needed to relax after that fiasco with my dress. Then I remembered that fine specimen of a mailman. I closed my eyes and I imagined him sitting on the side of the tub rubbing my shoulders. His strong but gentle hands kneading the muscles in my neck was releasing all of the tension. His hands slowly moving over to my shoulders and then forward cupping my round and modest breasts. I let out a soft moan as the vision played in my mind. I felt his hands move down toward my belly button and linger there for a moment then finding their way to—bzzz-bzzz, my cell phone vibrated.

"Damn it why does that always happen?" I answered it.

"Hello." It was my friend Tanya.

"Hey chick of the sea, what are you doing?"

I sighed and then asked her, "Why are you always calling me at the wrong time?"

She asked, "What are you talking about? I can call you back later heifer."

I laughed, "No it's cool I can continue what I was doing some other time."

She asked, "What were you doing?"

"Bath aerobics."

Her voice puzzled she said, "What the hell?"

I laughed, "Just tell me what you are calling about because I am in the tub."

There was silence for a moment. "Don't be mad but I can not go to the Christmas party with you."

First I received the wrong dress, then my hot fantasy was interrupted, now this. What in the hell was going on? My name is Janice not bad luck Sally.

I sighed again and asked her, "And why not?"

"I have to have surgery on my foot and that weekend I will be laid up in bed."

I pulled the phone away from my ear and looked at it as if I could see her. I put it back to my ear and asked her, "What happened to your foot? We were just together last night at the party dancing our tails off and your foot was moving pretty good."

She started laughing and said, "You don't remember? That's right you were pretty messed up. I was trying to help your toasted behind down the stairs and tripped my own damn self. I can not believe that you do not remember. You laughed so hard that you almost peed on yourself. It was hurting so badly this morning I went to have it x-rayed. It was not sprained but they did notice that a bone in my toe is growing crooked and they want to put in some type of splint thing."

I did not want to seem insensitive but couldn't that wait until after the party?

"Do your thing girl. I am a little disappointed but we can do it next year. Since your foot is not sprained maybe we can go over to Rockefellers tonight. You may as well party before you go out of commission."

We shared a little more conversation and said goodbye. The water in the tub was now chilly so I finished lathering up and got out. I went up to the third level of my townhouse where my clothes and shoes were. I had transformed the two bedrooms upstairs into my dressing room and walk-in closet. It was my own little boutique and I loved it. I had both a full length and a three-way mirror. In front of the three-way I had a pedestal to stand and twirl on. All of my friends thought that I was crazy but I did not care. This was all about Janice and if I had the means to do it why not? Don't hate the player just join the game—if you can. I needed to select an extremely sophisticated outfit to wear to Rockefellers tonight. Rockefellers was a club downtown in Georgetown. It was off of the chain. Everybody who was anybody would be there so my outfit had to be top of the line designer. After trying on about five different outfits I finally chose one to wear to the club. Then I selected another casual outfit to throw on in the meantime so that I could run a few errands. Once I was dressed I grabbed my purse and my sunglasses and headed out to the garage. Looking at my car I noticed that it needed to be run through the car wash. So that was first on the checklist. My car is just like my style. It is shiny, sleek, sexy, and totally seductive. My Mercedes Benz 600 series is no joke. It is fully equipped just like the men I date. The brothers are not the only ones who can have their stuff tight. That's right Sistahs are on the rise and we aren't carrying anyone else's baggage. The proof is in the pudding. And for those of you, who don't know the flavor, it's choc-o-late. I pulled into the car wash and as usual the brothers are trying to impress the vanilla honeys. I just smile and put the top up on my car. Unfortunately some of our brothers want everything easy. They can't appreciate it when the *sistahs'* want to excel. The saying goes stand behind your man. That's the problem. We've been standing behind them kissing their butts while they go out and spank someone else's. Believe me I learned that the hard way. Therefore any chocolate lover who wants to slide under my covers needs to realize he can walk beside me or keep on stepping. I may be a lot of things but easy is and never will be one of them. Speaking of chocolate lovers Rockefellers will be filled with them tonight. So the next thing on my checklist is to get my hairdo tight. After they finished the hand wax on my car I drove over to the strip mall to Hair 2 Dye 4. My stylist was truly to die for. She was the queen of hair stylist. Her prices were a little on the steep side but she was worth it and so was I. I never had to tell her what to do she just did it and I was never displeased. Just as I thought I left the salon looking magnificent. I also had my nails done while I was there so those two things I could check off of my list. I was beginning to feel my stomach growl so

He looked over his shoulder and then looked back at me. He shook his head and then said, "My apologies Janice McKane for disrupting your lunch and getting your red panties in a bunch."

Then he walked away. He had a lot of nerve. My old mailman was beginning to look pretty good right now. I finished my salad and headed home to get ready for the night's festivities. On the drive home I couldn't get the mailman off of my mind. I wanted one more opportunity to put his ass in its place. Who did he think he was? Gods gift to women? He wasn't all that cute. Well maybe he was. I turned on the radio and tried to release the thought of him from my mind. By the time I reached home he was replaced by the soothing voices of Luther and Levert. I went inside the house and listened to my messages, showered and changed. Tanya offered to drive and she was on time for a change. We got to Rockefellers about ten and already the place was packed. We partied until three and then we went home. It was about four in the morning when she dropped me off at home. It was about nine-thirty a.m. when the noise from the neighbor's lawn mower woke me up. It's Sunday doesn't anybody go to church anymore? I rolled out of bed and said my prayers. I know I should have been at church myself but every once in awhile I skipped. I lounged around all day and by the time Monday came I was rejuvenated. The week went by fast. Everyday I waited for the mailman to deliver my package. By the time Thursday came I was truly pissed. I began selecting my second choice outfit to wear to the party. I called the customer service department again but they could not tell me anything. Friday I left a note on my mailbox asking the mailman to leave the package with my neighbor because I did not want to take the risk of missing the delivery. When I arrived home from work I went straight to my neighbor's home. The package had not been delivered. Frustrated I began to think that maybe I should just skip the party this year too. I had already visualized how good I would look in that dress and I had my mind made up that it was the dress I wanted to wear. It was stunning. Oh well 'say la vie.' I went home and poured myself a glass of red wine and tried to mellow out my bad mood. I kicked off my heels and stretched out on the chaise lounge. I channel searched on the television until I came to the movie Miracle on 34th Street. I loved to watch old classics. I must have drifted off to sleep when the doorbell rang and startled me. I looked around and the room was dark accept for the light of the television. I glanced at the clock and it said ten o'clock p.m.

Who could this be? Tanya always called whenever she came by after eight. I went to the door and it was the mailman but he was not in uniform. What the hell was he doing at my house this time of the night?

I yelled through the door, "Can I help you?"

He said, "It's me your mailman. I have your package."

I was feeling a little nervous so I asked, "Why didn't you deliver it earlier today."

He told me that he had tried to deliver it but the neighbor was not at home and he held onto it because I had mentioned on the note how important it was for me to receive it."

I eased the door open and I said, "My husband is sleeping right now in the other room."

He laughed and said, "Is that why you said that your name was Ms. McKane?" Listen I am not some crazed pervert. I just wanted to do a good deed. If I could have gotten it here earlier I would have but they have extended hours at the post office for the holidays."

I looked at him suspiciously and asked, "I suppose you changed your clothes in the car?"

He laughed again shaking his head, "No I went home and changed first. My sister, who is in the car he turned and waved at her, is accompanying me to a Christmas Eve party at the Regal Publishing building. We are on the way there and I thought I would drop it off to you. So here it is thank you and goodnight." The girl in the car was the one from the restaurant. She was his sister. And not only that, he was going to the same Christmas Eve party. I was about to close the door when he yelled back.

"Tell Mr. McKane that I said, Merry Christmas."

They were not even away from the curb when I ran upstairs to get dressed for the party. When I entered the party everything looked beautiful. The decorations and the smell of the pine trees that adorned the room made it that much more of the holiday spirit. People were laughing and having a merry old time. I was scanning the room for you know whom. After about an hour I still did not see him. Maybe he had left already. I didn't think that I had taken that long to get dressed but maybe I had. Oh well. I went upstairs to the luxury suite to powder my nose. Then I heard a voice behind me.

"Is that what was in the package? If so I am glad that I went through all of the trouble?"

I turned around and replied, "Yes it is and thank you if that was a compliment."

He smiled and slowly approached me saying, "Yes it was a compliment and you look ravishing if I am allowed to say so. I would not want Mr. McKane to be upset thinking that I am flirting with his wife."

I couldn't help but to laugh and to say, "You know damn well that there is not a Mr. Mckane. And are you flirting with me?"

"Well that depends," He said.

My eyebrows furrowing together I asked, "On what?"

He stepped into my space and put his hands on my buttocks and said "If you wore the red panties?"

He kissed me and red panties or not this man wanted me and I wanted him. We found our way into one of the empty offices and right there on the desk of one of the CEO's we did the wild thing. I was hearing not just Christmas bells but all types of bells. There was passion mixed with the heat of roughness. I felt his hands and his lips. I didn't know which pleasured me more. He kissed me gently on my neck and then my shoulders. His hands cupped my breasts and found their way to my belly button. His fingers traced a circle and then proceeded downward between my thighs and they entered me teasing me until I felt the warmth of his breath and then the coolness of his tongue.

"There, there, oh right there," I moaned.

I felt the edge of the table dig into the arch of my back. I grabbed hold of his head and I felt the spasms between my legs. I quivered and screamed. When I didn't think he had any left to give he gently lifted me onto the table. He saw the surprised look on my face and he asked, "You've never heard the saying that the Postman always rings twice?" I closed my eyes and waited for my Special Delivery.

HAVING YOUR CAKE

Roland removed the wired hangers from the pole and tossed his freshly pressed shirts over his shoulder. He winked at the young girls standing behind the counter as they flirted with him as they always did. He was a weekly regular at the *Prim and Press for Less* Dry cleaner. They were the best cleaners in town and he knew that he could always count on a big hug and a kiss from the young ladies behind the counter. They waited for him anxiously each week at approximately five forty-five p.m. He loved the attention of his nieces and even though they could barely see over the counter they insisted on being the ones to wait on him when he came to pick up his freshly starched shirts. He extended his hand across the counter and handed each of them a twenty-dollar bill and told them to keep the change. They giggled because they knew that his dry cleaning was always free. They exchanged a blow of kisses and Roland turned to his sister who was now shaking her head because he always spoiled them. Roland blew a kiss her way and she pretended to catch it as if it had flown through the air. She pressed her hand not to her cheek but to her heart. She loved her brother. They had been thick as thieves since-well forever. Roland had been married once but his wife had been killed in a terrible accident. He had such a difficult time recovering from it all, in fact she had thought at one point in time that he would need to be committed. It was not until she told him that she was pregnant with her first child, which turned out to be twins that he showed some sign of wanting to live again. And though he would disagree, she knew that he loved life through her daughters. She wanted more for him. He had so much going on for him. He was smart, attractive, had his own practice and because he was a dentist he had a gorgeous smile. Women were around him all of the time but he had closed himself off. It had only been a month ago that he had taken his deceased wife's photographs from off of his desk. It had been six years since her passing. She had not told Roland but she had a surprise planned for his birthday. And even if he stayed mad at her for the rest of her life she was not going to change her mind about it. She turned to glance at her daughters who were now dancing around happily with their twenty-dollar bills as if they were the riches girls in the world. Roland returned to his car and glancing at his cell phone he saw that it had been on silent. He had two missed calls. He pressed the voicemail button on his cell phone and listened to his messages:

"Hello doctor Peterson, this is Trenia. I was calling to let you know that your 8:00 appointment has cancelled. I did not schedule anyone for that time in case you want to come in later. The phone beeped again with a second message: "Hey Uncle Roland, we are waiting for you." Roland smiled as he heard the girls smacking there lips making kissing sounds into the phone. He would die for those two just as he would have that night of the accident that took his wife away from him. Roland released the keys and let them dangle from the ignition. He let his head fall back onto the headrest and he sighed. He had no more tears and he was angry that he did not. He did not understand what was going on. How could he not still mourn someone that he had loved so passionately? It was his fault that she had died. He should have been home and not at the airport waiting for her in the storm. She had asked him to forgo going to the convention—"Just this once," she had asked him. Why didn't he just say yes? If only he had said yes she would be there in his arms. He traced his finger across his cheek but there were no tears. Where was the pain that he swore to suffer until he died? This was his punishment for himself. It was his fault that she was gone. Gone forever. He heard the tapping at his window and it startled him. He sat up and saw Trenia

He put the car in drive and sped away leaving Trenia standing in the parking lot with a puzzled and displeased look on her face. After a long hour and fifteen minutes Roland had made it home. He threw his briefcase onto the sofa and headed towards the kitchen but he could hear his wife's voice saying to him, "Roland please don't put your briefcase on the sofa. It squishes my pillows." He would always laugh and she would run from the kitchen and into his arms. He would grab her and pull her close grabbing her buttocks and locking them into his tight and loving grip. She would press her body into his and urge him to taste her sweetness beginning with her lips and then between her thighs. Dinner was always ruined because they could never stop once they began. She quivered as he bit into the cradle of her neck and gently suckling her skin leaving a mark of passion. Her nipples twanged as she anticipated his tongue finding its way to them and then being surrounded by his mouth. She purred when she felt his erection hard and long against her thigh. Her body moist with perspiration as his fingers felt their way up the mini skirt that she purposely wore for him. Roland wiped the sweat from his brow and took a few steps backwards until he was standing at the sofa and removed the briefcase. He took and placed it at the foot of the stairway. He felt and fell. Roland leaned his forehead on the banister as his vision slowly faded. She was gone and he had to let go. He just did not know how or if he could. The weekend had come and gone and Roland was back at work. He had seen at least twelve patients that day and they all needed at least one cavity filled. He was just putting his last case folder in his desk when Trenia came in.

"Is that all for today Dr. Peterson?"

Roland noticed a little curtness in her voice.

"About the other day Trenia, I know that you were trying to help me and I apologize for being a little short. I just had a lot on my mind."

Trenia cleared her voice and said, "That's fine Dr. Peterson. Don't let it bother you."

Roland looked at her and with a slight smile replied, "It can't be fine because you are calling me Dr. Peterson and we no longer have patients."

Trenia folded her arms across her chest and pushed one foot forward. "Well it seems that our relationship can only be professional so what else would I call you Dr. Peterson?"

Roland put up his hand trying not to be angry. "Trenia we had this conversation before and I told you that I am not ready for this."

Trenia took a step towards him. "Ready for what Dr. Peterson?"

"For this" he repeated making a wide gesture with his hands.

Trenia moved two steps forward. "Please be more specific Doctor."

Roland ran his hand across his forehead. "Trenia you know how much I loved my wife. I don't think that I can do it . . ."

Before he could finish his sentence Trenia was in his space and her breath was whispering across his face as she asked, "What this?" And she held his face in her palms and pressed her lips against his until he made way for her to insert her tongue. When she felt his apprehension melt she pressed her full body into his and moved him back to the edge of his desk. She was arousing him and that was half the battle. Now she just needed to get him naked. While still kissing him she unzipped his pants. She pushed them down around his hips until they were under his buttocks. She smiled to herself as she realized that Dr. Peterson—Roland wore briefs. Her heart pounding she put her hand inside of his unzipped pants and she felt all the glory of him. She without hesitation let out a soft moan and said, "Magnificent." She slowly moved down to her knees unsure that if he would stop her. He didn't. She squeezed his penis at the base and placed him into her mouth. He tasted so good to her. She had dreamed about this moment. She was taking him slowly and she was careful not to look at him because she knew that it was new and difficult. She had worked in his office long enough to know that he had loved his wife. No one would fill her shoes. Trenia was not trying to do that. She just wanted to share her love with someone that she hoped would some day love her back. Just as she was ready to bring him deeper into her throat she felt him grabbing at her shoulders. At first she thought he wanted more but he was pushing her away. Finally he pushed harder than he intended to and she fell backwards onto the floor. He reached out with one hand towards her apologizing while using his other to pull up his pants.

"I'm sorry Trenia, I can't. I just can't. I'm sorry," he said and rushed out of the office with his pants half zipped. Trenia sat on the floor not hurt but confused. She was not going to give up on him. She was too in love with him.

Friday had finally come and that Saturday was the surprise party for Roland that he was not supposed to know about. His two young nieces had unintentionally let the cat out of the bag. He really did not want all of the fuss but he knew that his sister was only doing what she thought was best. He also knew that she would invite every single woman in town. He would go home and get goodnights sleep because he knew that Saturday was going to be a long day. He walked out of his office and he was surprised to see Trenia still there. It was a Friday and she was normally gone way earlier than now. He approached her with caution because neither of them had spoken about the incident that had occurred in his office. He leaned over her desk; "You're working rather late for a Friday night?" Trenia stopped typing on the keyboard and turned towards him.

"Well I have a date and it would be senseless for me to go all the way home."

She stood up and took off her lab coat and let it slowly glide down her freshly bronzed arms. The black form fitting, bust pushing up and out dress that she had on gave Roland an immediate erection.

"I changed a few minutes ago." She pulled the lab coat back on and sat down and continued typing.

Roland adjusted his jacket in front of him and said, "Goodnight."

Trenia without stopping yelled across her shoulder, "Goodnight."

She smiled because she knew that she had given him a boner. Roland stood at the elevator and all he could think about was the mention of the word date. He did not understand why he suddenly felt jealous.

Saturday was just as he had expected. His sisters' backyard was full of women. Had she been collecting them all year he thought as his eyes roamed from one to the other. Then his mind started to weed them out.

"Oh no, Hell No and Not if I were the last man on earth No!" Roland thought that his sister had lost her mind and he was going to go and tell her. After battling his way through piercing eyes and wandering hands he made it to the kitchen door. Through the screen he could see Trenia. A flash of what she had been wearing the night before entered his mind. Her well endowed bosom, her thick curvy hips and that well-rounded ass. He shook himself back to reality and opened the door and went inside. Trenia hugged his sister and let out a "Humph," as she walked past him without so much as a happy birthday.

His sister stood and looked at him momentarily. She was curious about what had just happened.

His sister gave him a puzzled look. "What was that all about?"

Roland shrugged his shoulders. I think . . . I know that Trenia likes me."

His sister ran over too him, "Oh Roland that's great. I have always loved Trenia. She has always had your best interest at heart. When Toni died, Trenia was calling everyday to check on all of us. She was here with me sometimes when I needed someone to talk to."

Roland cleared his throat, "You could have called me."

His sister looked him in the eyes, "No I couldn't. You were in too much pain. You withdrew so far away that I thought that I had lost you too."

Roland rushed to his sister and held her close. He kissed the top of her head, "You know that I love you. I will never leave you and I will always be here for you now and forever."

She cradled in his warmth and she had to ask, "Please Roland, please won't you love again? Toni would want you too."

Roland did not respond but he knew that he felt something for Trenia. He was not sure what it was but he was no longer feeling the guilt of thinking of someone else. His nieces came into the room and before he knew it they had squeezed in for a group hug. Suddenly they began chanting, "We want cake! We want cake!" They all broke the embrace and Roland threw his hands into the air and said, "I guess we want cake." Roland had just turned towards the door when he heard all of the commotion. The largest cake that he had ever seen was being rolled onto the patio. They all stepped outside and Roland looked at his sister in disbelief. The top of the cake flew open and there stood Trenia nicely decorated holding a sign, "Happy Birthday Dr. Peterson." Roland smiled at Trenia and as their eyes locked they both knew that he was going to have his cake and eat it too.

QUIET OF NIGHT

You come to me in the quiet of the night your
arms embrace me holding me close and tight

I feel your pulsing heart race upon my skin
anticipated pleasures excuses all adulterated sins

I close my eyes to shed away the dawning of
early light knowing that morning will bring
reality to end all fantasies of the night

your eyes suddenly look apologetic
but your lips they fail to speak

but I know that it is time for you to go by
the sweet kiss you place upon my cheek

I watch as your contented shadow slips
away as cunningly as it came in

and I await the Quiet of Night to be
your mistress once again

THE PROMISE

Tiffany sat on the edge of the bed and watched as Eric dressed to leave her. This was a ritual that they went through every other weekend of each month. She sat quietly on the edge of the mattress that just moments ago conformed to their two entwining bodies. Her mind was speaking loudly within her head with all of the thoughts of becoming Mrs. Eric Dennison. Sometimes she wondered if they were loud enough for Eric to hear. She wanted to speak up and to tell him that she wanted and needed more from their relationship. She wanted him to know that being his mistress was no longer pleasing or respectful enough for her. Yet she refrained from saying anything at all for fear of what the outcome would be. Tiffany did not know how much more she could take of him leaving her alone and going home to be with his wife and children. Eric had always been honest and open with her from the beginning. He made it clear that no one or any circumstance would take him away from his family. So when they began the relationship they promised each other it was strictly recreational and that neither one of them were looking for commitment. It was to be simple with no complications. They would enjoy each other sexually and go on with their individual lives. But after two long years Tiffany wanted to be Eric's full time partner. After All she had earned that much hadn't she? She kept him entertained with the latest talk about sports and current events. She cooked before he even asked her to and the sex was off of the chain. In fact it was so damn good she did not understand why Eric was not doing the same things to his wife. But isn't that the role of the mistress to make the man believe that he can not get the same gratification from his wife. Tiffany knew that she had to stay on top of her game so she had to plan her strategy and use it at the right time. The last thing she wanted to do was to push him away. She watched as he buttoned his shirt and tucked it down into his freshly dry-cleaned trousers. He felt her starring at him and glanced over his shoulder to look at her. He turned back towards the mirror and smiled. Tiffany smiled back and then she ran her tongue across her lips. She placed her hand on her thigh and she winked at him. She then parted her legs just enough for him to see her intimacy. Moving her hands towards her womanhood she licked her lips again but much slower and seductively. Eric watched her from the mirror and that heightened her arousal. She brought two of her fingers to her mouth and suckled them until they spread wide as though she were going to be examined by a physician she licked her inner fragrance from her finger and then moistened her clit. She was ready for Eric to devour her. He stepped closer to her and dropped his wrinkle free trousers to the floor where his knees proceeded to fall on top of them. He placed his hands beneath her buttocks and brought her closer to him. He sniffed her scent and the aroma brought his lips to her vagina. He kissed what pleasured him and then he slid his tongue into her opening and teased her. Tiffany's body squirmed and she moved forward to meet all of his tongue. She loved the way he orally sexed her. He was never too fast or too slow. His movements were precise and creative. He was an artist and his tongue painted the strokes that sent her body into multiple spasms. He would suckle her clit and then push his tongue deep into her. She could feel his saliva mixed with his sweat run down between her buttocks. He would then place a finger into her anus but never leaving her clit or vagina unattended. She called his name over and over again. In fact she wanted to call his name each and every night. Tiffany grabbed Eric's head and pulled him further into her. She wanted his tongue if at all possible to be deeper within her. She was begging him to taste all of her. She made the mistake when she whispered to him, tell the 'little wife'. She got great satisfaction from knowing that she had not only screwed Eric but his wife also. In fact it turned her on. She took his penis deep into her throat and she suckled him until she felt his cum trickling down her throat. Eric had her head between his hands and he did not know what to do. He did not want the pleasure to end because he wanted to feel her moist softness surround his long hard penis. He wanted to flip her over onto her stomach and take her from behind until she begged him to stop but he could not because she was pleasuring him too much. Eric's knees buckled and his face tightened as though it were in a vise. He took a few deep breaths and fell forward pushing Tiffany backward onto the bed and collapsed on top of her. She cradled him in her arms until she felt his breathing come to a slower pace.

She asked him, "Are you alright?"

Eric only moaned and squeezed her breast. She chuckled and held him tighter. After a few moments he raised his head to glance at his watch. He did a double take and jumped up almost detaching Tiffany's arm from her shoulder. Tiffany yelled in pain, "Ouch damn it!"

Eric looked at her and realizing what he had done he reached out to rub her arm but she angrily snatched it away from him. He looked puzzled for a moment then he said to her, "I'm sorry, I just realized what time it is and I am late. I need to call my wife so she won't worry or become suspicious."

Eric waited for Tiffany to agree but when she did not he went to the dresser and retrieved his cell phone. He hurriedly dialed his home number and turned to Tiffany placing his forefinger to his lips he motioned for her to be quiet. Tiffany listened as Eric told his wife that he loved her and that he would be home soon. She held back the tears as he looked into her eyes with no uncertainty as he told his wife, "Only you, I promise." Tiffany sat on the edge of the bed and watched as Eric dressed to leave her.

THE BOX

The crowd was small but growing larger as the music from the saxophone became more intense. He was blowing that saxophone as if he were in a moment of passion and imagining himself being blown. He was straining to give it his all. He held onto the note as though he was reaching his climax. The crowd loved what they were hearing and they applauded and whistled. I just loved what I was seeing. The brother was fine and his form-fitting shirt told the story that he was built just right also. I listened to the notes as they blew across the sky and I imagined my fingers playing them across his chest. The performance ended and he announced that he and the other performers would now be taking a break. I immediately went into plan mode. I had to think of a way to casually introduce myself but make a lasting impression at the same time. I looked down to give myself a quick glance over to make sure everything was intact and that the girls were in the glad to meet you position. Yep, everything was just picture perky. He finished his selection and moved off of the stage. Some of the other people in the crowd were approaching him also which meant that I might not get to talk to him before his break was over. I waited patiently for the others to take their turn speaking to him and then I made eye contact. We both seemed to smile at the same time. He was even more gorgeous up close. He had a tan that said that he had recently been to the Islands. I was hoping that it was not with the wife. One thing that I can say proudly about myself is that I do not under any circumstances do anything with married men. Even as fine as his black ass was I would have turned and walk away. I quickly looked at his tan fingers and searched for the clue of where a ring may have been. There were no signs of a ring but I kept in mind that he could have removed it before he had gotten the tan. I extended my hand and introduced myself. He graciously accepted it and he even held onto it for a few moments before letting it go. Suddenly my plan of attack failed and I felt myself becoming bashful instead of aggressive, which is usually how I am.

He finally spoke and asked the question, "Are you enjoying yourself and my music?"

I twisted my lips as if I had to think for a moment and then I smiled and responded, "My answer is yes to both. That is why I walked all the way over here to tell you that I truly enjoyed your playing."

He laughed and said, "All the way over here. I think you were pretty close. I saw you when you first came up the pathway. I noticed how you plowed your way through the crowd."

I know that I was blushing but I was going to stand my ground. "Well I saw the crowd forming and I did not want to be too far in the rear. I like hearing the music but I also like watching the performers."

He put his hands above his shoulders and stretched his body.

He came back to his original position and asked me, "You're not one of those groupies that follows bands around are you?"

Now I'm thinking that this guy is going to be an asshole and he is obviously stuck on himself. I thought to myself, what a waste of damn good chocolate. He must have read my mind because then he said,

"Hey I was just kidding around. I am nobody famous and I know I play well but I am not stuck on myself. I love my music and myself but I need someone else to love me too. I did not mean for you to take that so seriously."

I tucked my hair behind my ear and lied telling him, "Oh I didn't. I knew you meant it to be funny."

The grin on his face told me that he knew that I was lying. We both laughed. He asked me to stick around until he finished the second half of his performance and I did. This man had a lot to offer. I could tell that by the way he played his saxophone. I was hoping that later that night I would be hitting a few high notes of my own. After the show was over we talked a little more and exchanged numbers. He had volunteered to play that afternoon to help raise money for the Miami Fire Department. I made a mental note to add a few extra dollars to my donation check the next time. I was delighted to find out that he was and had not been married and did not have any children. His nine to five was at an accounting firm in downtown Miami. I worked as a paralegal in Fort Lauderdale. We decided to walk down to the little *Tikki Bar* where we continued to sit and ask questions about one another. Time flew by before we realized that we had been sitting there for three hours. It had been a beautiful afternoon and now the evening sky over looking the canal filled with ducks and geese was breathtaking. Palm trees lined the shore in the distance along with skyscraping high rises and cruise ships. The sun was warm and the breeze blew the mist from the canal onto my skin that felt refreshing and cool. Donovan Michaels was his name and he was very handsome, intelligent and charming. We made plans to see one another that following Sunday. Donovan wanted to get together sooner but I insisted that I was too busy with things that were job related to commit. I knew that he could have taken me home and had his way with me but I was not going to be a one night roll in the hay although it had crossed my mind. He walked me to my car and gave me a gentle kiss on both of my cheeks and we said goodbye. I had given him my card with all of my contact information on it and I was hoping that he would call me that night but he didn't. I even thought about calling him but I decided to wait and not be the aggressor this time around. That next morning when I arrived at my desk there was a box wrapped in a yellow bow. I opened the attached note card and read the message:

> *If you trust me you will not open this box until you are with me.*

I did not know what to think. I had just met this man and he was asking me to trust him. I picked up the box and I shook it gently. There was definitely something inside. At first I was a bit agitated but then I decided to play along. All day I kept trying to guess what was in the damn box so I finally removed it and put it somewhere out of sight. When I got home I put on some soothing music and poured myself a glass of wine. I turned on my computer and checked my e-mails. Halfway through my reading I received an IM from Donavan.

> *You did not call me so I am going to assume that you are going to trust me. Trust is beneficial to any relationship and I am glad that we are off to a good start.*

Okay this guy was beginning to freak me out a little. Even though he did have a valid point I was still a little leery. I decided to do a background check to take a little peek to see who he really was. Everything checked out okay but that still did not mean that there were not any loose screws rolling around under those dreads. I now wanted Sunday to come and to be over with so that I could move on. The workweek seemed to go slowly by and for most of it I was preoccupied.

Saturday finally came and I had not received any more messages from Donavan. I knew that we were to meet at the *Tikki Bar* again near the park on Sunday at two o'clock but I was curious that he did not call to confirm anything. I wondered if that was part of this trusting gimmick that he had going on too. I went into the living room and removed the box from the closet and placed it on the table. There it sat on my table with its beautiful bow and wrappings. I walked over to it and stared at it. I wanted to open it. I stared at it some more as if I thought I would eventually see inside of it. I picked it up and put it to my ear and I shook it as I had done before. It was the same. I held the end of the bow in my hands and fiddled with it for a moment. I told myself to open it. I wanted to but I couldn't. I cursed and put it back down on the table and left the room. I could hardly sleep that night wondering what the hell was in that damn box. Sunday morning finally came and the sun shining through the window gave me the impression that it was going to be another glorious day. I took a long luxurious bath with lots of bubbles and scented candles. I tried to think of anything and everything other than that box. I laid my head back onto the bath pillow and closed my eyes and thought of my upcoming afternoon with Donovan. My thoughts weren't sultry though they

<u>The Black Pearl</u>

Unlike any other

A rare specimen of fine and unique quality

I turned the card over and read what he had written on the back of it.

*If you are reading this note then there is no need for you to meet me. I am looking for someone that I can trust in my life and with my life. Please keep the jewelry box because without any doubt you are a diamond. However I can buy **Diamonds** wherever I go. It is the **Black Pearl** that I am trying to find.*

Donovan

RECKLESS

I eased my foot from the gas pedal as my Mustang convertible took the curve going 60 miles per hour. I knew that I was taking the curve too fast but the thrill was exciting and the danger of it all made me feel alive and awake. My hair full of curls danced about my face almost blinding me. The car began to slow down just as it entered the heart of the curve. The driver in the huge tractor-trailer that was on the opposite side of the road sounded his horn. I threw my hand over my head and waved. I could not have been in a better place in my life. Everything just seemed to be in the right order. I looked to the right of me and the mountains were gorgeous. The sun beaming down on my body was an organic aphrodisiac. I pushed the button on the steering wheel and changed the CD. I needed to hear something mind blowing. This was the life. The life I had waited forty-five years to arrive to. I was finally able to stop and smell the roses and not only that I were able to purchase a few. My move up the ladder had put me in a pleasant financial status. I was not rich by a long shot but I was definitely comfortable. And by comfortable I mean I could buy without justification. Just two short months ago I had to decide whether to use my last dollar to buy a loaf of bread or a dress. But I was finally able to sell my designs to a buyer and now I am on my up. I turned the CD up and let the music pump as fast as my car. I was in it to win it. I grew up in a family of six. We were not poor but we always seemed to struggle. My mother always wanted better for us and she did try to give it to us. She always thought that I would succeed in life and she pushed me hard to do just that. Of course I fought her all of the way. I was a little hellion. She wanted me to be feminine and lady-like. I wanted the exact opposite. I loved hanging out with the guys and giving them high fives and patting them on the ass. I never dressed up or cared about make up. If my brothers were playing football I was in the game too. Hell I played better than they did. Eventually my mother won me over. My senior prom I promised her I would change my ways. She had become ill with cancer and I knew it had always been her dream to have a little princess. I put on the make up and the girlie gown and wowed everyone including myself. I actually surprised myself because I learned to like what I saw. I began to design my own outfits because my body was a little awkward. I had curves but they were not all in the right places so clothes from the mall never fit me just right. I did not always have money for tailoring so my doughboy had nothing on her. I would not be at all surprised if she had not flown in a jet to get to the mall. Yeah it was like that with her. Even though she had it like that she was still down to earth. She was the most giving of the three of us. I thought about that for a few minutes and made a mental note to myself that I needed to give back more. Pam was the fly girl. She had bank too but she loved the rendezvous. She needed a lot of sexual healing. She could sweet-talk the stripes off of a tiger. And believe me she had dated a number of them. She was absolutely gorgeous. I am talking about men would stop dead in their tracks and just look at her. She absolutely hated the attention. She was kind of shy but she loved the hell out of sex. I think she had an addiction but I enjoyed her telling us all about her little sexscapades. In fact I had used a few of her techniques in my own boudoir. Of course I would never let her in on that little secret. We ended the night a little early because Pam had an early call in the morning. Normally we would be out until we saw the sun coming up. Now that I was back on straight highway I put the pedal to the metal. I was easily doing seventy-five. I had not seen a car in the last forty minutes so the road belonged to me. I was on the back road and not many cars traveled on this side of the mountains mainly because of the tractor-trailers you been drinking ma'am?" He asked me to step out of the car and I followed his orders. I closed the car door and he grabbed my wrist and turned me away from him in one forceful move and shoved me against the car door. He released his grip from around my wrist and his hands moved my skirt up and around my naked behind. He took his Billy club out and smacked my buttocks. That heightened my arousal and I moaned. He pulled me backwards so that I could feel his erection. I took the club and tossed it into the seat. I was on fire between my legs and I was not in the mood for games. He was just the opposite because he whipped out his handcuffs and locked my wrists together. He unzipped his pants and took out his manhood that was as long and thick as the club that lay on the seat of my car. He held my skirt with one hand as he used his other one to grab my hair and with one thrust he entered me. The feeling of his thickness was so good. He moved in and out of me. The metal of the car rubbed against my clit bringing more excitement. I arched my back and tried to position my buttocks so that he could enter me further. He moved one of his hands to the front of my body and massaged my clit. I wanted to touch myself but I was handcuffed. I was at his mercy. I begged and begged for him to go deeper. He complied and I licked my lips as I imagined

TOO MANY COOKS
IN THE KITCHEN

The black wrought iron pan that was on the stove was hot and filled with sizzling strips of bacon. My mother stood over it humming her favorite spiritual. She had her hair pulled back into a simple ponytail and she was dressed in one of her oldest cotton dresses. You wouldn't know that she and my father ran a successful business. They loved living the simple life but they knew how and when to be extravagant too. She was not a fancy woman but she was regal. I often stood and watched her. She would always somehow know when I was standing somewhere near her.

Without turning around she asked, "And how are you this morning Miss Sibbie?" My name is Sylvia but she insisted that I should still be called by my childhood nickname. I would laugh and ask the same question I had always asked.

"How did you know that I was here?"

She would always give the same answer. "I always know when there are too many cooks in the kitchen."

233

That meant I needed to get out and let her do her thing. Her kitchen was her domain and you did not enter it when she was cooking without her request. But my mother knew that this particular morning I needed to be requested to come in. She turned and looked over her shoulder at me.

"Come in and sit down. I am a good listener if you need me to be."

Before I could answer the tears fell. My mother did not move and I couldn't. She turned the pan off and removed it from the burner. She went to the refrigerator and took out a large pitcher of orange juice and then went to the cabinet and took out two tall glasses. Without a word she motioned for me to sit at the table. She met me there and poured us both a drink. Placing her hand on top of mine she simply said,

"I could tell you that everything is going to be alright but I can not predict that. But what I can tell you is that no matter what it is I am here for you. Whatever burden you are carrying you do not need to carry it alone."

The words were all jumbled in my mind. I had rehearsed and rehearsed what I would say and how I would say it. She waited patiently until finally I spit the truth out.

"Mama I am pregnant."

She said, "Child I thought you had bad news. I have been waiting five long years to become a grandmother."

The smile of happiness that came over my mothers' face was quickly replaced with concern when I began to cry openly as if I had told her of someone's passing. Tears began to well in my mothers' eyes.

"What is it, baby please tell me what it is. Let me help you with this burden no matter how heavy it is."

Through a shower of tears I looked at my mother and I told her.

"I am pregnant but the baby is not Franklin's."

I felt the strong grip of my mothers' hands slowly release themselves from mines. Suddenly everything seemed to be moving in slow motion. She raised herself up from the table and returned to the stove. I watched her for a few moments. I did not know whether to speak or not to speak. I wanted to move but I was afraid.

She stood there silently and then turning to face me she asked, "Who is the father?"

I did not want her to know. I did not want her to pass judgement on the man I had fallen in love with. I did not want her to criticize what she knew nothing about. But I had come to her and to not tell the truth was no longer an option. I spoke almost in a whisper, "It's Daniel. Daniel is the father."

My mother looked down at her feet and folding her arms across her chest she slowly raised her head to look up at me. She repeated his name as if she weren't quite sure that she had heard correctly. I waited for the storm to erupt. I wanted her to lash out and to scream obscenities. This is what I had prepared myself for when I came into the house this morning. I had prepared myself to say good-bye to the woman who I had loved all of my life and who had loved me.

She looked up to the sky and said, "Lord you are going to have to help me with this one. Please help me to understand because I do not want to forsake my own child."

I wanted to go to her and wrap my arms around her. I wanted her to know how sorry I was. I needed her to know that I had fought hard and long with my heart to say no to him but my love, our love was just too strong. I wrapped my arms around my body and I began to rock myself in the way my mother had always rocked me. I wished that I could change what I had done but at the same time I was exuberant with the joy of bringing another life into the world. Our baby his and mine. My mind began to play different scenarios of Daniel and I together as a happy couple, unlike my husband Franklin who insisted that we never have children because they would only be a burden to him and his career. I loved children and I wanted to have a lot of them. I wanted all my holidays and birthdays to be shared with the laughter and love of children. I knew that I could never be fulfilled in such a way with Franklin. Franklin was my parent's dream. He made them happy and I settled. For five long years I settled so they could all be happy. Daniel came into my life and for the first time I knew who I was. I knew what I wanted and needed. Unlike Franklin, Daniel put me first. He was always making himself available for me. His focus was on our happiness and not just his. I remembered the first night that I met him. It was at a Christmas party that my mother had for her office staff. As usual I was there helping her. I loved being her sidekick. She called me the '*hostess with the mostest*'. Daniel was there. He was tall and slender. His skin was a beautiful chocolate brown and his eyes had me memorized the moment I looked into them. He was impeccably dressed from his smooth shaven head to his Italian leather shoes. Talk about a Christmas delight he would have made the perfect gift for under my tree. However I was married to Franklin and we did have a commitment. Daniel could only be a fantasy. I began helping my mother out for other numerous activities that related to her job. The more time I spent at her office the more contact I had with Daniel. My mother and father had their own real estate company and they were preparing for a large open house. My mother had a few last minute items that she needed to be picked up so she asked Daniel if he could accompany me over to the warehouse. We were to pick up another dining room table to place in the formal dining area of the home that she would be showing. After we picked up the table and had it placed in the house, Daniel and I decided to take a little private tour. The house was spectacular. We entered into one of the bedrooms and we were both in awe. We both looked at each other and it was as if we both had the same thought. There could be a hell of a lot of loving going on in that bed. The images began to make me fidget and I was becoming uncomfortable and hot. I began wondering if Daniel was seeing those same sexual images in his mind. I knew that I wanted him too. In all of my fantasies he had been in them. I cleared my throat bringing us both out of our trance and we moved onto the next room. This room was more exquisite than the previous one.

I turned to Daniel and said, "Maybe we should head back downstairs and make sure everything is in its proper place for the showing."

He took a long look at me and then asked, "Why did something suddenly make you uncomfortable?" Lying I told him "No, I think we have seen enough and besides my mother will be wondering what is taking us so long."

Looking as though he did not believe me he responded with, "If you say so."

With a questionable look on my face I asked him, "You don't believe me? Why would I have reason to be uncomfortable?"

In one single motion he swept me up in his arms and pulling me closer to him he said, "Because of what I am about to do."

He placed his lips on mines and with the urgency of my wanting his tongue to enter my mouth I parted my lips to let him in. We kissed with such passion I had forgotten my commitment to Franklin. But what was more frightening I no longer cared. We made our way to the bed. I am not sure if we were still fully clothed when we got there but by the time that I felt the silk sheets caressing my skin I was already on my way to my second climax. Every movement he made he found a new place to create ecstasy for me. I did not refuse any of what he was offering and he was pleased with that. Moments went by and we lay there in each other's arms.

I asked, "What do we do now?"

He tilted my chin upwards so that he could see into my eyes and he said, "Buy new silk sheets."

Coming back to reality in my mother's kitchen she was still standing at the stove. She had removed the bacon from the pan and was now preparing to scramble the eggs. Her silence filled the room with awkwardness and prolonged my agony. I could not take it any longer. I stood up to leave and she began to speak.

"I met Daniel at a real estate convention in New York. He was very handsome and quite the charmer. He was top notch in the industry and I immediately knew that he would contribute to the success of our business. We had dinner that evening and we discussed his interest in joining our company. At first I didn't think he would be willing to relocate but after about our third meeting he was more excited than I was. I arranged a meeting with your father and Daniel and they hit it off right away. It did not take anytime for Daniel to move up the ladder in the business because he had already educated himself to a level beyond our expectations. When he received his first big promotion your father and I wanted to take him to the Golden Plaza for a VIP dinner. Your father was called away that morning to give a lecture for one of the realtors who had become ill. Your father insisted that Daniel and I should still go. We did and we had dinner and then drinks. There was a live band and we decided to dance. When the evening ended we should have gone home. We should have said goodnight but we did not. I had never been unfaithful to your father. I had never thought about it or had even been tempted by it. It just happened. The next day Daniel came into the office and he was so happy. He thought that we were going to continue being intimate. I tried to explain to him what I could not explain to myself. He was so angry. I tried to tell him that I was sorry and that I had made a terrible mistake. I was willing to take full blame and we did not have to tell anyone. But he was hurt and embarrassed but mostly he thought he was going to lose everything. I tried to convince him that he had done nothing to jeopardize his job but he wouldn't believe me. Everyday when he came into work he would come to me and threaten to tell your father. And everyday I would assure him that his job was safe. Finally I could not handle the secret anymore and I told your father the truth. He forgave me and told Daniel that he should move on and not make trouble for anyone. He sent Daniel to another company where he would make twice as much money. On the last day for Daniel to work for us he came to my office and he said to me, "You will regret this," and then he walked out. Ever since that day I have been looking over my shoulder waiting for the worst to happen."

My mother turned around and I heard the eggs hit the hot skillet. As she stirred the eggs I watched the spoon turn around and around and around. So many thoughts began to enter my head. I did not know who to be angry with. I walked over to my mother and putting my arms around her I held on tightly for a moment. I then kissed her on her cheek and as I felt her tears fall onto my arms I told her good-bye. As I turned to leave the room my father entered and with his usual smile and delightful attitude he asked,

"And where do you think you are going?"

Not sure if I knew the answer to the question I replied to him,

"I don't know dad. But what I do know is that there are too many cooks in the kitchen and we have all been burned."

WHO'S WATCHING WHOM?

The night air was filled with a mysterious coolness. It had a sense of secrecy about it. I pulled the shawl around my bare shoulders as I headed down the alley towards home. I could hear the sounds of horns blowing and screeching tires and then faint curses of obscenities from motorist who had obviously had too much to drink. I pulled my shawl tighter around me as the chill of the wind caught my skin as it blew across me. The alley was dark and not a safe place to be but it was the shortest distance to travel when I was going home. Normally I would have taken the bus but I had missed it due to the fact I had miscounted the money in my register. I could have stayed and waited another hour but the crowd at the bar would usually become more rowdy and out of hand as the night went on and I was not in the mood to be fighting off drunkards who felt that my buttocks were a free for all. The Dumpster smelled of old trash and food as I hurried passed it and headed to the pathway that led into the park. I heard a sound of what I hoped was the wind rustling among the bushes. I stopped to listen again. The sounds were faint and as I moved forward cautiously I realized that they were human whispers.

At first I thought that it was one person. I prepared myself to run and to go into the other direction but the light from the lantern that swayed with the wind cast a hint of two bodies that were entangled. I knew that I should have moved along but I was intrigued and suspicious. They did not seem to notice that I was there. Maybe they did and just did not care. Perhaps they were not filled with the inhibitions of being on public display that most of us wished that we did not have. Or maybe the darkness of the evening had surrounded them enough to convince them that they were shielded from the light that had cast a glimpse of their shadows. I watched as he pulled her hair away from her face and gently placed indiscreet kisses on her neck. Her hands pressing into his back as she bit playfully at the lobes of his ears urging him on. He laughed and from what I could hear his voice was rough and masculine. She taunted with him as he tried to reach beneath her dress trying to snatch her goodies. He would run his hand along her upper thigh and she would playfully push him away. But he was not discouraged by her actions. He kept pursuing her until she grabbed him by his shirt and pulled him towards her. Her lips parted and his tongue forged in as if he wanted to reach the back of her throat. She must have wanted him too because she raised one leg and was trying to escape. She unzipped his pants and took his bulge into her hands. She massaged it between her palms as her tongue licked the tip of his manhood. At first her movements were slow and erotic, as were mine as I touched myself. Then as though she had read my mind her movements became fast and greedy because she wanted all of him. I wanted him. He held the back of her head holding her prisoner. He moaned and he moaned and he moaned. She took his manhood fully into her mouth. The deeper she took him in the wider I opened my mouth. He threw his head back. She swallowed and I swallowed. He placed both of his hands beneath her skirt and removed her panties. He pushed his tongue into her. He licked her most sensitive spot over and over, around and around and she squirmed digging her fingers into his shoulders. My breathing became heavier as I found my own sensitivity. He lifted her buttocks from against the wall and he entered her. He slid his thickness into her wet mound and I slid my fingers into my own. His thrusts were rhythmic and I mimicked his movements with my fingers. I fondled my breasts squeezing them and pulling at my nipples. I imagined his teeth biting at them and his mouth covering them as he suckled. I spread my legs and begged myself to find that magic spot. I wanted him to leave her and come to me. I

KEEPING SECRETS

He sat across from me at the table making me feel
what I had not felt in quite some time it was hard for
me to keep my sinful thoughts in place
I feared he might be able to read my mind

tracing his lips with my eyes
I heard not a word that he spoke
too busy wondering how his hands would feel how
gentle and tender his strokes

watching him smile and flirting with me
was more than I could stand
I was definitely captivated and longing to be here
with this man

wishing that he had sat beside me
his closeness I would have embraced
perhaps given an opportunity
to sneak a seductive kiss upon his face

taking his hand beneath the table
leading him to what he needed no permission to do
letting him know that I can keep a secret
I know that he can too.

STICKY BUNS

I had just enough time to run into the house to shower and change. I was going to have lunch with an old friend today and I wanted to be sure that I looked good. I had not seen him for awhile so I was genuinely excited. I threw the car keys on the counter and rushed up the stairs kicking my shoes off as I went. I pulled my tee shirt over my head and pushed the sweat pants to the floor and stepped out of them. I had just run a few miles and I was hot and sweaty. My reflection in the mirror told me to keep doing what I was doing because I was *'Looking good'*. I turned on the shower and stepped into the tub. I pulled the clip from my hair and let it fall to my shoulders. I stood under the running water until every inch of me was wet inside and out. I lathered myself with the lavender soap and inhaled its' aroma. I palmed my breasts until they were covered with soapy bubbles and I tugged at my now erect nipples. I stood under the showerhead and let the water flow steadily over my body. As it trickled down between my thighs I felt its sensation as it gently teased my clit. I gapped my legs and arched my back so that I could feel the intensity of the steady stream. I lifted my head so that the water flowed over my head and down between my breasts as if they were rolling hills. The water trickled through my fingers that were now moving up and down and in and out of my most precious possession—my valley. I braced myself against the shower wall as I brought myself to a climax. I let the water continue to flow until I could breathe normally and lathered myself again. After showering I went into my walk in closet and picked out an outfit to wear. I selected a tight fitting short denim jeans skirt and a sheer lace top that had a little flirty flare at the bottom. I smoothed lotion and cocoa butter all over my body and then embellished it with a sweet scented perfume. I then put on a pair of high-heeled stilettos and I was ready to go. He called my cell phone but I did not answer. I intended to be purposely late so that I could make my grand entrance. Just as I had hoped he liked what he saw. He was still as handsome as ever. Not much had changed about him at all. I was a little intimidated by that because now I was worried about how much he thought I had changed. I was older than he was so I hoped that he would not notice my aging. I felt good and I thought that I still looked good as hell but that was my thinking. If he felt differently he did not say anything. We sat at a quiet booth towards the rear of the restaurant. The waiter came and took our

He looked at me and asked, "Are you all right?"

Giving him a little lie I just said, "Yes. Its' just that this seat is getting a little hard."

He lifted my leg with his under the table until he had my foot in his lap. He removed my stiletto and placed my foot on his bulging penis and asked, "Like this?"

I should have never mentioned the word hard. I glanced down as if I could see his penis under the table and cleared my throat. I am a shy girl by nature so I slowly looked around to see if anyone was checking us out. But I reminded myself that I needed to step outside of the box. Stop being so uptight. So I answered him by playfully massaging his manhood with my toes. After a few moments he got up and came to sit next to me. As sexy as I had ever heard any man he whispered in my ear, "I want to taste you."

I did not say anything; I could not do anything. When his warm breath and sensual voice hit my earlobe I knew that all of my shyness had gone out of the window. His presence being that close to me sent chills down my back. It was all that I could do not to get up and strip down to nothing. I pulled myself together and muttered, "Here???"

Before I could say anything else his finger was between my skin and my thong and just a knock away from entering my front door. I felt my legs, which should have been closing, open a little wider. With his left hand he picked up a sticky bun and fed me while his right pushed the door open. With my mouth full of sticky bun I moaned and everyone in that restaurant thought I was having the best thing I had ever eaten. I slid my hands under the table and as unnoticeably as I could I placed it on top of his. He leaned in towards me again and whispered, "You liked that huh?"

He knew that I was already too far-gone to speak so I just nodded. He then took my hand and placed it into the opening of his pants. I wondered to myself, when did he open his pants? This brother was smooth. I fondled him under the table while he fed me more. He leaned in and kissed me and I felt his tongue lick the icing from the sticky bun which was on my bottom lip. He fed me another piece and I felt his fingers move into me deeper. I kissed him and suckled his tongue. I imagined his tongue taking the place of his fingers. I wanted him to be beneath the table and sucking my insides out as he grabbed onto my own sticky buns. We stopped kissing and made small talk for appearances sake. He began pressing against the tip of my clit with his thumb and I moved my body forward so that I could feel the pressure of his fingers on my G-spot. Our breathing was heavy but we maintained control. I released his penis and I grabbed the napkin to cover my face as I felt the intensity of my orgasm. I squeezed my thighs tightly around his hand until I felt them quiver. I placed the napkin in my hand and returned it to his erect penis. He picked up his glass of iced water and held it to his lips and pretended to drink as I whispered naughty little nothings into his ear. I watched as his brows furrowed inward as if he was getting brain freeze as he ejaculated. He left the well-seasoned napkin in his pants and pulled up his zipper and excused himself to go to the bathroom. When he returned the waiter approached the table asking, "More sticky buns?"

We looked at one another and smiled.

AS RIGHT AS THE RAIN

Yvette was exhausted. She had just done a double shift at the hospital and her body as well as her mind was drained. She walked down the long hallway towards the illuminated sign that pointed to the exit and she debated on whether she should walk down the three flights of stairs or wait for the elevator. She was so tired that her legs gave out at the door of the elevator. She fell back against the wall and propped her body against it. She closed her eyes what seemed like only a minute when she felt herself being shrugged. She opened her eyes and Brian was standing in front of her with a devilish grin on his face.

He touched her cheek, "That was good for me. How was it for you?"

She slapped his hand away and she looked around to remind herself where she was. She then looked back at Brian, "Very funny. I must have dozed off. What are you still doing here?"

Brian glanced at his watch and replied, "I still have about an hour left then I get to dump this joint. You want to wait around and catch something to eat?"

She shook her head and covered her mouth as she yawned and said, "No I don't think so. Anyway you know I don't play around with someone else's man."

Yvettes' friend Tammi was crazy about Brian and she was not going to break their friendship code by going out with him.

Brian looked back at her and with a scowled look on his face he told her, "I am no ones man. I keep telling you that I am not interested in Tammi. Whatever she keeps telling you or whatever she thinks is going to happen is false."

Yvette put her hand up to his face and said, "Whatever."

The elevator doors opened and Yvette stepped in. As the doors closed she waved goodbye to Brian. She pressed the down button and the elevator moved. Yvette thought about Brian and she wished that she could have taken him up on his offer. She herself had longed to be with him but Tammi had spoken for him first so she kept her feelings for him to herself. She and Tammi had been close friends for years. So close that they considered themselves as sisters. Yvette would not betray that trust for the love of any man. There were times that Tammi would call her and tell her about the conversations that she would have with Brian. And even though the majority of them sounded one-sided Yvette would never tell her. She also would never tell her of the dreams that she had about being with him. She could not tell her of the fantasies that would leave her in a heated sweat at night. No she could never tell her best friend that she was in love with her man. Regardless of what Brian had told her he was Tammi's man. Yvette pressed the button on her keypad to unlock her car. She was almost at a running pace to get to her car. She could not wait to feel the cushioned seat on her bottom. She was just that tired. Turning on the ignition she backed the car from the parking spot and headed towards the exit gate of the garage. Once outside it was a blinding rain. Yvette was too tired to fight her way through the madness. She pulled around the corner and found a parking spot in the deserted maintenance parking lot. She would wait for the rain to clear up a little and then she would head home. She made sure that she had locked herself in and she let her head fall backward against the headrest. She felt herself nodding and she thought that she should just rest for a moment before getting onto the road. Her eyes closed and she drifted off into a deep sleep. The rain continued to fall heavily and Yvette continued to sleep until she turned her body and hit the horn on the steering wheel. She jumped bringing her body and her mind to full attention. She looked around and barely being able to see out of her window because the rain was still coming down in a steady pour she turned on the windshield wipers and she could see the outline of a body heading towards her car. Her heart began to race and she fumbled with the keys in the ignition. She turned the keys with too much force and instead of starting the car it made a whining sound. She turned the key again and this time the engine started and just as she was about to put it into drive she heard her name being called. She kept her foot over the pedal as she pressed the button to let her window down just a tad. She heard her name again and she recognized the voice. She put the car in park and left the engine running. Brian approached the car and she put the window down.

He peeked inside and asked her, "Yvette are you alright? What are you doing parked over here? Did your car break down or something?"

He was asking so many questions at one time that she could not answer any of them. The rain was pouring all over him and his face was covered with raindrops. Yvette unlocked the door and motioned for him to come around to the other side and to get in. Brian ran around the car and opened the door and got into the passenger seat. His drenched shirt hugged his body allowing his six packs to be seen. Yvette followed his chest up to his eyes and she wanted to kiss the raindrops from his sexy lips but she knew that this was a no-no. Brian wiped his face with the tail of his drenched shirt exposing his wet skin. Yvette felt chills run along her spine. He looked at her and he asked her again what she was doing there. She turned off the engine and explained to him how she was trying to wait out the rain and that she had fallen asleep. He scolded her and told her that she was not thinking and that she had put herself in a dangerous situation. She did not appreciate the way he was speaking to her and she cut him off in the middle of his sentence, "Excuse me," I am not a child. I know how to take care of myself. I appreciate your looking out for me and all but I am not five years old."

Brian raised one eyebrow and looked at her. His look made her uncomfortable because it told her that he knew that she was not a child. That she was a woman and he wanted to show her just how much he knew that. Yvette cleared her throat and looked away from him and looking out of the front windshield she said, "Looks as if the rain is not going to let up anytime soon. I am going to go on and go home."

She looked back at him, "Thanks for coming to my rescue even though I was really ok."

She touched his hand lightly. Brian smiled at her and waited for a moment to see if she would ask him to stay but when she did not he ended the silence and spoke, "Well I guess I will see when I see you." He opened the door and stepped out. Yvette watched as he ran across the front of the car and headed across the parking lot. What in the hell was she doing? She opened the door and she felt the rain cover her all at once. She yelled out to Brian but he continued to run away from her through the rain. She called his name again this time louder. He turned and stopped looking back as if he were not sure what he had heard. He took a step back towards her direction and then another step until she was clear in his vision. He picked up his pace and ran back to her. Standing in front of her with the rain covering his face he asked her,

"What, what's wrong Yvette?"

Yvette did not speak. She looked at him and answered with her eyes. Her eyes told him that she wanted him. That she had always wanted him. Tammi entered her mind and she blinked her away along with the raindrops that lay on her eyelids. She tried to tell him but no words would come out. He grabbed her into his arms and he kissed her. She tasted him along with the rain and it felt good. He ran his fingers through the wet strands of her hair as he kissed her face and neck. He reached down and unbuttoned the first few buttons of her blouse loosening it enough so that he could pull it over her head. She lifted her arms and the rain fell over her and she felt as if she were dancing in the rain. He unhooked her bra and her breasts were exposed to him and the rain. It was cold and she could not tell if it was Brian or the rain that made her nipples erect. Perhaps it was both. He kissed them as the raindrops splattered onto them sliding between his tongue and her cleavage. He pressed her back against the car and she felt the cool metal against her back. She pulled his soaked shirt away from his shoulders and down and around his bulging muscles. He was beautiful. He wiggled his arms from his shirt and let it fall to the ground. He took her into his arms and he held her there momentarily. He slid his hands to the hem of her skirt and raised it up and around her hips until her panties were exposed. He pulled them down until she could feel the cool air at her opening. The sensation was gratifying as he entered his finger inside of her. She moaned as he took her tongue into his mouth as he kissed her. She kicked her panties that were down at her ankles off and wrapped her leg around his thigh so that he could have full access to her jewels. She was as wet as the rain inside and out. Brian loosened his belt and unzipped his pants. Yvette blinked her eyes to remove the raindrops so that she could have a clearer vision. When Brian removed his pants he was magnificent. Yvette squeezed her thighs together to keep herself from having an orgasm just from the sight of him. She wanted to taste him. She placed her hand on his penis and the silkiness of his skin was so smooth that she could not help but to caress him. She pulled him towards her and turning his body so that he was now leaning against the car she pushed him back and she slowly went to her knees and resting them on his pants she leaned forward and took him into her mouth. She teased the tip of his penis as the raindrops fell to her tongue. She tasted the salt as she wrapped her mouth fully around his erect penis as she suckled him. The rain pummeled her head as she took him to the back of her throat. Brian held onto her hair as the rain streamed down his chest and onto his manhood for her to taste. When he could take no more he pulled her up and they switched positions and he kissed her again. Brian lifted her and carrying her to the front of the car he placed her onto the hood. Yvette rested onto her elbows and watched as he spread her legs so that he could taste her. He teased her opening with his tongue and the coolness of his breath mixed with the pulsation of the rain sent her mind into frenzy. She fell back onto the car and let him have his way with her. Her body squirmed as he licked and darted in and out of her. He placed his hands on her hips and pulled her forward. She put her arms around his neck and waited for him to enter her. She moaned as she felt the smooth snake slither into her wet opening. He moaned as he felt the juices of her tight walls encumber him. Each move that he made was slow and precise. She dug her nails into his buttocks urging him to go farther. He listened to her commands and acknowledged them. He made love to her until she needed more. They were both beyond the passion. His rhythm becoming faster. His grip became tighter. The rain falling harder. They came. Brian fell forward onto Yvette and she held onto him. Yvette knew that tomorrow she would feel the guilt of the wrong that she had done. But now in this moment it felt as right as the rain.

A TOY STORY

Troy pressed his body firmly against Shayla as he placed the strand of magnificent pearls around her neck. He loved to feel the roundness of her buttocks against his manhood. He was so proud of her and each one of the pearls that adorned her long and lean neck told her so. He tugged gently at them as he clasped them together making sure that they were securely fastened. Shayla marveled at them and at her man as she stood in front of the mirror. The man who stood behind her was her life and she treasured him just as much if not more, than the pearls that graced her neck. She touched them with her hands and she knew that she would never forget this moment. She turned to her prince and kissed him passionately. He lifted her into his arms and carried her to the bed decorated with soft rose petals and satin sheets. He laid her down and looked upon her as if this were the first time that he had seen her in the raw. It felt that way for Shayla too as she blushed like a schoolgirl. Troy had been her first encounter and as far as she was concerned he would always be her only encounter. He sat beside her and leaned forward until he was only a breath away and he kissed her lips lightly as if he had just blown a feather. He kissed her chin and followed the curve of her neck applying small gentle kisses as he went along. Shayla touched his hand and he took hers into his until their fingers were interlocked. Troy could not get enough of this woman and he would love her in a way that would leave her breathless and satisfied. He stopped kissing her just long enough to tell her, "Shayla, I love you more than love." She reached to wipe the tear from the corner of his eye and she raised her upper body from the pillow that cradled her head and she threw her arms around his neck. She held onto him tightly as she told him, "There is no love for me without you." Suddenly there was nothing in the room but the two of them. It was as if they were suspended into the air. Only their two naked bodies holding onto one another for life. The room was silent with the exception of their quiet sniffles. Troy placed his hands gently onto her shoulders and eased her back onto the bed. He straddled his body over her and this time he kissed her long and hard as if this would be his last time. Shayla waited to receive him. He kissed along the side of her neck with his mouth open just slightly enough for her to feel his warm breath on her neck. He stopped as he reached the cradle of her neck and he suckled her there inflicting just enough pain to arouse her. She let out a soft whimper letting him who would throw her ass against the wall and spank her and tell her naughty nothings as he fingered her. She breathed heavily into his ear and she grabbed her breasts and pushing them together she pushed them against his mouth. Troy looked at her and he saw in her eyes that she wanted more tonight than he had ever given her. He did not know what had gotten into her but he liked it. He began to lick and suck the mounds of flesh as if they were his last meal. Shayla placed two of her fingers in her mouth and moistened them and then she played with her nipples. Troy watched the show as she fondled her breast for him. She returned her fingers once again to her mouth but this time she placed them at her secret passageway and teased herself. Troy looked at her and all he could say was, "Damn baby its' like that?" Shayla smiled at Troy. She spread her legs further apart and moved her hips and moaned calling his name. He wanted to touch her but he also wanted to see the show that she was putting on for him. She moved one hand to her breasts and she played with them kneading them and twirling her nipples between her fingers she arched her back and wiggled her buttocks feeling the softness of the rustled satin sheets. Shayla stopped momentarily and pointed her finger towards the nightstand. His eyes followed her finger and he reached across and opened run across his vein adding more sensation. She teased the tip of his manhood and sucked it until she felt the muscles pull in her jaws. She placed the now vibrating tongue against his balls as she joined in with her own. She took him again in her mouth her jaws tightly gripping him until he threw his head back and called her name. She released him and they came face to face and she kissed him and she repeated his words to him, "I love you more than love." He in return responded, "There is no love for me without you." He rose up on his knees and pushing her legs apart he placed his tongue in her. He tasted her and he kissed her there letting her know that she was beautiful and he was thankful for what was in front of him. He caressed her inner thighs as he gently teased the tip of her clit before he suckled it. His tongue caught her moistness as it drizzled down from her garden. He was passionate and accommodating with his lovemaking and she could not wait for him to enter her with his manhood so that they could ride off together. He stopped but not until she begged him. He flipped her over and he entered her from behind. He placed his arm around her so that he could grab her breasts. His other arm was around her upper thigh so that he could pleasure her from the front as he entered her from the back. She leaned forward onto the

"How many times do I have to tell you Harvey I don't wanna' play hides and seeks with you!"

I stood up and stomped my foot and headed into the house. Harvey stood up and started to follow after me until I turned quickly towards him ready to kick him in the knee. He looked at me as if to dare me and then he said, "Maybe you will feel like playing tomorrow." He stood there waiting for an answer even after I shut the door in his face. I did not look back. And when I graduated from high school I did not look back. The day after I walked across the stage to receive my diploma I left. I left it all because I wanted more. I wanted so much more. I had saved just enough money to get a train ticket to nowhere. And nowhere was Atlanta Georgia. I did not know anything about Georgia but Georgia did not know anything about me so I thought that it was fair. I was barely legal and out on my own. I was not scared because I did not have time to be scared. I had a lot on my agenda. First I had to find a place to live. Then I had to find a job so that I could remain at the place where I lived and last but not least I needed transportation but the bus and subway had to do for now. I found a little room to rent by the week. It was not much to look at but it had potential. I looked around and thought the first thing that I needed to buy would be a disinfectant. And a plant would help to liven up the place. It was home and it was mine, tentatively speaking. I bought a newspaper along with the plant, a bottle of bleach and some milk and cereal at the corner store. I walked the three blocks and looking at the freshly landscaped lawns it felt rather cozy. And the people that I passed by seemed friendly enough. I placed the plant in the window and put the other items away and sat down at the little round table to read the want ads. I circled a couple of possibilities and then I decided to take a light nap. I must have really been tired because it was almost dark when I awakened. The other renters must have come in because I could smell the aromas of food and I could hear voices and sounds from radios and televisions. I stood up and stretched and pulled my hair up and twisted it into a knot. I yawned as I reached my arms to the ceiling. I looked up and I spotted an insect.

"Oh no!"

I looked around for something that I could use to kill it. I did not have a broom yet so I pulled the chair away from the table and stood on it. I removed my shoe and swiped at it and it crawled a few inches. I swiped at it again and this time it fell. I looked down at the floor and I did not see it. It had fallen on me and I stared to jump and shake and the next thing that I knew I was falling out of the chair. I tried to balance myself but it was too late and as I felt myself falling I shouted, "Oh S-H-I-T!"

The chair fell over and I fell over top of it. I thought I had broken my ribs. I lay there for a minute and I heard a knock at the door. I tried to catch my breath as I pulled my shirt up to check for bruising.

I yelled out after they knocked again. "Who is it?"

The voice behind the door was deep and husky, "Are you alright in there?"

I had not realized that I had made such a commotion but I yelled back, "Yes I am. Thank you."

The footsteps after a few seconds led away from the door and I heard the screen door from the front entrance slam shut. I slowly raised my body up and headed into the bathroom. I just wanted to soak in a long hot bath. The warm water felt good against my skin as I eased down into the tub. I must have eventually drifted off to sleep because when I awoke to sounds of knocking the room was dark. I was still sore and as I eased out of the tub I knew that it was going to be painful to get out of bed the next morning. I dried myself off and threw on my white terry cloth robe. I heard the knocking again but this time there was shouting that went along with it. I heard a woman's voice shouting obscenities. Whoever Derrick was, he was in for one hell of an ass whipping. I walked over to the door and peeked out of the peephole.

I could see the back of the woman but not her face. She was tall and slender and her hair fell just above her shoulders. She continued to knock and curse for a few moments more until another roomer opened his door and asked her to politely move along because she was interrupting his evening news program. She placed her hands on her hips as if she could give a damn and then she asked the elderly man if he knew Derrick. The elderly man looked back at her and told her that he had not seen anyone in that apartment for the last month. She did not move. She asked the elderly man again as if she had not heard him correctly and then she kicked the door. She fell against the door and slid to the floor.

The elderly man shook his head and said, "You young girls will never learn," and then he closed his door. I returned to my room and left her to her misery. I did not know who she was or who Derrick was but I suspected that he had made her promises and had left her wanting more. A familiar story that I myself knew too well. After six months of mulling through the newspapers and endless job interviews I was ready to tuck my head between my tail and return home. I had packed just about all of my belongings and was about to buy a train ticket with my last few dollars when I received a call from one of the jobs that I had interviewed for. The person that they had hired had not worked out that well so they wanted to offer the position to me. It was not my dream job but it was a job none the less. It would keep my rent paid and put food in my belly. I unpacked and selected my outfit for my first night on the job. I stepped into my heels and ran my fingers through my hair and checked my red lipstick to make sure that I had not applied too much or too little. I sat at the table and watched as the hands of the clock moved slowly about its face. When it was time for me to go I pulled on the black double breasted trench coat and hung my black patent MK look-a-like bag over my shoulder. I hailed a taxi and instructed the driver to take me to my job location.

The hotel was grand. My heels clicked as they glided across the freshly polished marble floor. My shoulders back and standing tall I approached the front desk as if I was a resident there. I told the clerk with confidence as I stared her in the eyes, "Key for room 527 please."

She stared back at me and I wondered what the problem was but then realizing I had not given her my name, I apologized and repeated my request but this time adding my name, "Ms. Devereau."

She then eased the tension in her eyes and smiled and handed me the little enveloped that contain the key card. I turned and with my eyes wandering quickly to find the direction of the elevator I headed towards them. The doors opened and I breathed a sigh of relief when it was empty because I suddenly needed to catch my breath. I pressed five and the doors closed and the elevator went up. When the doors opened I went in the direction of the arrows that pointed towards 527. I stood in front of the door and I ran my fingers through my hair once again. I untied the knot in my coat belt and undid the buttons. I pulled it open so that the black lace teddy was exposed. I looked down to make sure that the little satin ribbons that formed two perfect little bows across my nipples were still laced and then I knocked on the door only once and then inserted the key card. I slowly opened the door. The room was lit with what seemed to be a million candles. The aroma of fresh cut flowers and incense was welcoming. A tall figure approached me and he reached out his hand and I took it. He pulled me in and pushed the door close with his foot. He put his hand on my shoulders and removed my coat letting it drop to the floor. He placed his hand across my throat and pushing me gently against the back of the door he pressed his face in the side of my neck. His breath was warm as he caught the tip of my earlobe and said in a firm voice, "I want to fuck you. I want to make you scream." His other hand had now made its way between my thighs and was pulling at the closure of the teddy. I was surprised that he was so patient with the closures because his language was savage. Once he was done he pulled the teddy up and around my waist. Using his knee he spread my legs further apart. He massaged my opening with his entire hand before he finally entered me with two of his fingers. He growled into my neck asking me if I liked it and I played along with him. I massaged his penis and grabbed onto his buttocks with just enough pressure to get his approval. He moved his hand away from my buttocks were in the air. My body became tense. I was fearful of what he was about to do but he must have felt my apprehension and he massaged my back. He placed small kisses along my back that led him to my butt cheeks. He gently but firmly clenched his teeth around my flesh and then released me. He slapped each spot that he nibbled on with his hand causing a slight stinging sensation as it hit my moist flesh. He was like a kid in a candy store and I could tell that he wanted to do anything and everything to what was for sell. He kept massaging, nibbling and spanking me until he had his fill. He turned me onto my back and spreading my legs open he pleasured me again. He entered me with a quick thrust and I heard him growl and press hard against me. I waited for him to move. He pulled back slowly and I felt his limp penis brush across my skin. I stood up and gathered my clothing. He came and met me at the door. He helped me put on my trench coat and as I tied the belt pulling it tightly around me he eased the folded money into my pocket. He reached down to kiss me but I stopped him and I turned and opened the door. I walked down the hallway to the elevators and pressed the button to go down to the lobby. The doors opened and I stood for a moment and watched the people in their expensive clothing walk across the marble floors. I watched the Mercedes, Rolls and the Lamborghini's as they pulled up. Yes I knew about wanting more and I planned on getting it.

ON THE REGULAR

Sheila pressed the round red button on the remote to her forty-six inch flat screen and cursed under her breath. It was Friday night and she was furious that her date had stood her up. And if to make matters worse she could not find one thing of interest on the television. She was paying almost two hundred dollars a month for her cable bill and not one channel was showing anything worthwhile. She tossed the remote to the side and she fluffed the pillow behind her back that had sunken into the corner of the extra large sectional sofa. She was so bored that she wanted to scream. She had been looking forward to the date all week. She had not been out with the opposite sex in quite some time and her insides were itching. She had told herself that she was giving herself some *'Me time'* Well that me time had lasted almost two years. She had just lost interest in platonic relationships. She had traveled to a few exotic places and had met some very handsome men but she had kept them all at bay. She was trying to put her life into perspective and she had put sex on hold and love in the backseat. Now that she was successful, in shape mentally, emotionally and physically she was ready to give herself completely. She just needed the right partner. She felt that she was the whole package and she could not understand why a good man was so hard to find. But no matter how hard it was she was going to take it slow. In the past she had often thrown herself into anyone who was packing a good eight inches or more. Sheila smiled to herself as she reminded herself of her last romantic encounter with Karl Whitman. But that was all they're relationship had been. Just sex and as far as romance, yes he did wine and dine her on occasion and she had reaped a few benefits such as diamonds and gold. But he too had benefited. He was getting great sex without commitment. Even though the relationship, as well as the sex had been on the regular it was not going to be anymore than it had been. He was the one who had made her take a good long hard look at herself. Maybe she needed to stop giving away the milk for free and let someone buy the cow. Speaking of good and long and hard, Karl was just that. When they had been dating, Sheila could not go a full day without wanting some of this man. It did not matter where she was or whom she was with. If the very thought of him crossed her mind she would break out into a sweat and often would have to excuse herself to go and bring herself to an orgasm. On a couple of occasions when she had been out on the visualized Karl standing in front of her naked and lean. That devilish little grin of his that he would always expose when he waited for her to suckle him. He would stand over her with all of his magnificence and wait for her to part her lips. He always tasted so good. He made sure that he was always so well groomed for her. That in itself was a turn on for her. He knew that he had to be on point if he expected her to bring it. She tossed her head to the side as she imagined her tongue sculpting the tip of his penis and then making its way down his shaft to his balls. He was very sensitive there so she would be very cautious to use just the right amount of pressure. Her hand would stroke the base of his penis as she moved her tongue back up towards the tip and this time she would take him all the way into her mouth and using her jaw muscles she would suck and squeeze until she heard him moan out loud. She inserted two fingers into her wet vagina and she ran her tongue across her lips, as she tasted him in her thoughts. She pressed her fingers deeper into herself as she saw images of herself grabbing his buttocks and digging into his mounds with her fingernails as she pressed him closer to her face. She took him deep until she could feel her lips touching on the lower part of his belly. She deep throated him once maybe twice, never more than that with the tip of his penis. It felt so good and she wanted all of his thickness between her thighs but he continued to tease her. He grabbed her breasts and pushing them together he licked her nipples simultaneously. He was rough and he knew that she liked it this way. She dug her nails into his buttocks so that he would know that he was getting the job done. He returned his tongue to her vagina and he devoured her. She cried out as he licked her over and over again. She felt herself coming and she grabbed his head so that he could not move from that magic spot. She screamed out and her body shook. He raised up and pushed his erect penis into her. She was so wet that it slid in like butter. She felt him swell as he rode her deep and hard. Her muscles tensed and she felt her second orgasm coming. She threw her legs open wider and let him have his way. He grunted as he held her ankles. She tried to free herself because she wanted to squeeze her legs around him but he was in control. She called out, "Oh God! Oh Karl!" He grunted one last time and fell across her. She squeezed the muscles of her vaginal walls together and trembled. Sheila opened her eyes and looked at the silent television. She removed her hands from inside her panties and cursed, "Damn you Karl!" For a brief moment she thought about calling him just so that she could get her freak on but she knew that ship had sailed. She needed to move on to bigger and better men. If bigger could be possible. She needed to be in a relationship where she could be on the same page. She was ready to be in a committed relationship without the drama. She just had not realized that it would be so difficult. Maybe she needed to stop thinking that there would not be a match for her in her bed like Karl. Sheila stomped her feet against the padded carpet as she headed upstairs toward her bedroom. She stripped down to her bikini lace panties and stood in front of the mirror. Her nipples were still firm and stood at attention. She touched her right one and pulled gently on it. She let out a soft moan. She then pulled at her left one and moaned again. She grabbed both of them with her hands and pressed them together as she moved them around and around. She slid her feet into the red stilettos that she had tossed there once she had found out that her date would not be coming. She turned her body from the right to the left as she continued to caress herself. She imagined that Karl was there sitting on her bed watching her. She began to gyrate her hips and push out her buttocks. She bent over and let her breast dangle as she squeezed and pulled at her nipples. She asked her imaginative spectator, "Oh you like that?" She reached behind herself and slapped her buttocks. Then she grabbed them and as she stood she released them. Looking over her shoulder towards the bed she jiggled her butt cheeks. She placed her fingertip in her mouth and she winked at her imaginary friend. She slowly turned and walked towards the bed and again she asked, "You want this? She pointed at her vagina. "You want this right here?" She stuck her entire finger into her mouth and moistened it. She placed it against her vaginal opening and massaged herself. She moaned as she crawled up onto the bed. "Oh I know you can do better than that." she said. She reached into her nightstand and pull out her pink toy. She pressed the on button and it began to hum and the pearl beads inside of it began to slowly flow up and down. The little rabbit ears began to vibrate rapidly as she increased the speed. On her knees she inserted the vibrator with one hand and she massaged her breasts with the other. She pushed the vibrator in and out of herself in a slow motion. She raised one knee from the bed and placed her foot there so that she was now in an h position and she looked down to see her opening. She imagined that Karl was beneath her licking the sweet juices that flowed between her. She pushed and twirled the vibrator between her flesh. She fell over onto her back and she turned the vibrator to its'

TEMPORARY INSANITY

Moments of awkward silence
then the tears fell
my mind trying to comprehend
what your lips had to tell

not wanting to look at you
knowing that I would recognize who you were
the man who I had given my everything
choosing to be with her

when did I become blind?
my eyes did not focus so that I could see
the deceit and the betrayal
that stood directly in front of me

my heart beating fast
first from anger than propelling into rage
you stood there waiting for applause
as if you were an actor performing on a stage

the hate that stormed inside of me
it was all that I could do
fall to my knees and pray
Heavenly Father forgive me for what I am about to do

the smirk on your face was putting salt into the wound
but I would have the last laugh knowing that this
would all be over soon

fingers reaching for the gun you insisted that we keep
beneath our bed now embraced in my hands placed
directly at your head

I give you my life and my love
in return you give me disrespect
temporary insanity overcomes me
then seconds too late remorse and regret.

She cursed silently reminding herself that she was not alone and yet she really was. Her mind drifted as she looked up at the ceiling. It drifted back to the years when she had first met her lover, the man of her dreams. It had been eight long and lustful years of hot and steamy lovemaking. He had been her first. She remembered the day vividly. It began with the two of them meeting for a casual lunch. He was dressed in a brand new pair of designer jeans and a form-fitting shirt that showed off his muscular arms. She remembered how when he spoke she could not help but to look at his pearly white teeth against his tan complexion. She could smell his cologne as though he was standing there beside her but he was not. She could feel the way he had touched her hand as they laughed jokingly about nothing. She clasped her hands together as she visualized how it happened that day. But she would no longer touch his hands, kiss his lips or make passionate love to him again. They would never have that first night again. They drove along the quiet highway under the stars and listened to the romantic music on the radio. Once in awhile they would sing if they recognized the song or remembered the words. When he had taken her back to her apartment she asked him to come in for a nightcap knowing all along what she wanted to happen. While he sat on the sofa she slipped into her bedroom and lit the scented candles that mimicked her name—Jasmine. She unbuttoned her crisp white linen blouse just enough to expose her lace bra and then she called to him, and he came slowly the way she wanted him too. He did not speak he just seduced her with that gorgeous smile as he removed his shirt to show his brilliant body. She waited for him and there he stood in all of his glory. He was amazing and she wondered if she had bitten off more than she could chew. No of course not. In fact she was not going to be chewing at all. When he approached her he took her hands and placed them around his waist. He lifted her chin so that her lips met his and he kissed her. Not with urgency but with a gentleness that said, "I won't hurt you. I will never hurt you." He pulled her blouse away from her shoulders and kissed each one. He pulled her sleeves over her hands and let it fall to the floor. He reached his hands around to her back and unhooked her bra. He slowly pulled it down away from her breasts as if he were unwrapping a fragile package. He looked at them and then into her eyes and his eyes spoke to her. She felt beautiful because he made her feel that way. He lifted her and placed her on the edge of the bed and pulled her skirt from around her waist and down her hips. He raised her legs just enough to remove it over her stilettos and then he gently pushed her back onto the bed. His lips found her navel and made little kisses all around. His breath on her skin gave her a powerful sensation between her legs. It was similar to the feeling she would have when she used her vibrator. But this was real. She could only hope that the sensation, the magnitude of her orgasm would be the same. He found his way to her thighs and she moaned because it tickled her. He glanced up for a moment to make sure that she was all right and she looked at him as if to say, "Don't you dare stop now!" He continued on his path until his lips found her lips the ones that lay waiting eagerly between her thighs. Her heart was racing because she was ready to feel what she had only read and heard about. "Oh, Oh!" she cried out. He parted his lips and placed his tongue there and it danced and she moved her body to the rhythm. It was nothing as she had imagined. There was no way possible that she could have imagined anything that would feel that good. She wiggled beneath him pulling away when she felt it too intense because she did not want to have an orgasm. She wanted him to be inside of her when she came. He played with her a little longer licking her and teasing her with his tongue until she cried out for him to stop. He pulled needed to be sure that they were really there. Her mind drifted back to the bedroom where she laid cuddled in his arms as he told her how beautiful she was. He promised that she would have many more nights with him and that each one would be like the first time. And for eight years he kept his promise or did he? When she found the hotel receipt in his jacket pocket she thought it was from a business trip. But when the hotel called to say that his wife had left her earrings behind in the back of the safe in the room where they had slept, she was not so sure anymore. She waited patiently until he had another business trip and this time she did a little detective work. And what she found out was that her lover was like all other lovers. He was unfaithful. She thought that she could handle it because after all they had not gotten married. Technically she did not have a bond with him under the eyes of God, did she? Eight years is a long time to give someone your life. She wanted to get married but he insisted that they finish college and then it was grad school and then let's do it next year when we have more money. All the while he was having his cake and eating it too. For weeks she followed him. Sometimes she would sleep in the rental car and call him while he was with her just to hear his lies. It made Jasmine sick to the stomach. Something inside her had snapped. And she knew it. She also knew that she needed to leave but her mind was telling her that was just not an option. She turned on the soft music and lit the candles that were the scent of her name and she undressed. She did not put on any lingerie only her red stilettos the ones she had worn that first night when he told her that she was beautiful. The night she gave herself to him in exchange for promises that he would never keep. She heard him enter the door and she waited. He walked in and as usual he was ready to make excuses about where he had to go, but not tonight. He made love to her. She made sure that he gave her what she needed and what she wanted. And for a moment, just for a moment she sensed his guilt. For a moment she thought he would do the right thing and tell her. The right thing would have been for him not to be unfaithful at all. He held her in his arms until she made him release her. He went into the bathroom and showered and when he returned she was sitting on the edge of the bed. The revolver was on her lap. He stopped in his tracks and looked startled before he gathered himself enough to ask, "Jasmine what in the hell are you doing?" She looked through him and answered, "You don't need to go tonight because she is no longer there. He looked at her and again he asked her, "Jasmine what did you do?" Jasmine picked

LOOK BEFORE YOU LEAP

Elisa did not know what was coming down heavier—the rain outside of her window or the tears from her eyes. She had closed herself away from everyone in hopes to avoid all of the embarrassment, humiliation and the numerous "I told you so." She glanced over at the one of a kind wedding gown trimmed in ivory lace and pearls that hung gracefully from its' sateen hanger. The wedding gown that her grandmother had spent the last few months diligently fussing over because it had to be a perfect fit on Elisa's curvaceous body. Elisa had been fitted so many times that she was afraid to eat for fear that her grandmother would begin making the gown from scratch if it did not fall just right over her hips. Her grandmother was so happy and proud that she had lived to see the day that her granddaughter was engaged and soon to be married. She was also honored that Elisa had chosen her to make her gown even though she had not always voiced a positive opinion about her soon to be significant other. She had told Elisa on more than one occasion; "Honey I know he makes you happy and all giddy inside but something just doesn't sit well with me about that boy. I can't put my finger on it, but you be careful. Just because you love a fool doesn't mean you have to be one."

Elisa would just laugh at her grandmother and she knew that she meant well. Her grandfather had not been the best of husband's and Elisa assumed this was why her grandmother was so over-protective. Elisa ran her grandmother's words around in her head. She did not think that her grandmother knew how much she would treasure what she had done for her and even though she would not be wearing the gown after all she would keep it forever. Her mother knocked at her door. She hoped that Elisa would allow her to come in. "Elisa honey, it's me your mother. Please won't you let me come in? Just for a moment?" her mother pleaded. She hoped that her youngest child would let her embrace her in her arms and help her through her pain.

Elisa just looked at the door and then she looked away. She could not face her mother. She could not face anyone. Today she had to be alone. She did not try to wipe the tears away from her face she let them fall freely. She stared across the lawn that was adorned with all of the fresh flowers and colors of spring. Spring was her favorite time of the year and that is why she had chosen the first day of the season as her wedding date. It did not matter to her whether or not the date fell on a weekday or weekend. She just knew that she had to say, "I do" on that date. That date had come and gone twenty-four hours ago but she never got the opportunity to say, "I do." It was silly but she had rehearsed those two words over and over in front of her mirror. She wanted them to sound just right when she said them to Brian. She wanted them to sound as sincere as they floated from her lips as they did when they remained silently in her heart. She could not have loved him more. She loved him completely without any conditions or reservations. Even when others continuously told her that he was not the one for her. That he was not Mr. Right but Mr. Wrong. She loved him and no one could change her heart or her mind. She had fallen in love with him the first time that she had looked into his deep dark brown eyes. They held such mystery and intrigue. hey were both in the downtown public library when she had piled on too many books and on her way to the table she dropped a few of them onto the floor. While everyone else looked on as if she were a klutz, Brian came to her immediate rescue. She remembered the strong scent of his cologne. It was manly and woodsy and complimented his physique. He was not muscular but you could see that he kept himself in good nostrils as if he were standing there in her room. She closed her eyes and took in a deep breath. She felt her hands touch his face. It was smooth except for the thin moustache that shadowed his upper lip. She kissed his cheeks. One and then the other. Stopping in between to place one on his full seductive lips. As she proceeded to repeat the step he caught her and suckle her bottomed lip. Then he slipped his tongue so cleverly into her mouth and kissed her deeply. His kiss was wet and savoring. Elisa opened her eyes and there was no Brian. That night of dreaming had since past. She was still sitting in front of her window. It was still raining and her heart was still filled with the pain. Again her mother knocked asking to come in. She told Elisa that she needed to eat. She reminded her that she had not eaten since yesterday morning. It also reminded her why. Yesterday was that first day of spring. Elisa wished that her mother would just let her be. She knew that her mother loved her and wanted to comfort her. But that was not what she wanted now because she knew that along with her mother's comforting would be some lesson. Her mother knocked again this time Elisa's patience caught the best of her and she yelled out, "Damn it mother please leave me alone!" She heard her mothers' footsteps disappear as she went down the hallway away from her door. Elisa felt bad about how she had spoken to her mother and her instincts told her to go and apologize but she couldn't. She could not move because she knew that the pain would follow her. It did not matter whom she was with or where she went this pain was like concrete. It was there to stay. It was solid like the love that she had for Brian. Solid like the words that he had repeatedly told her each and every time that they had made passionate love. They're first time being in the rear of the library after the poetry reading. She remembered how afraid she was at getting caught but at the same time being so excited. He had been teasing her all night long. Kissing her on her neck and grabbing at her breasts and trying to place his hand between her thighs when he thought that no one was looking. By the time the poetry reading was over she was well heated by all means and Brian was ready to bring the heat to a full flame. After everyone had moved to the front of the library Brian pulled her to the rear. His hands went beneath her skirt and he pulled her panties to the side so that he could slide his finger into her wetness. Her back pressed against the books and her buttocks heaved against the edge of the metal bookshelf he whispered nasty thoughts in her ear of what he wanted to do. She knew that this was not the place but his warm breath made her chest rise in her throat. He wanted to take all of her forcefully but the bookshelves rocked with each thrust so he had to be cautious and gentle. Elisa grabbed onto Brian's' backside and digging her fingernails into him she hoped that he would ride her hard. Each time he pulled back his return would come back deeper and deeper. Then she felt him at her most sensitive part and she gritted her teeth and pressed down harder onto his penis until they both were almost onto the floor. Holding onto him as she tightened her muscles around his penis as she climaxed. She buried her mouth into his neck to muffle her scream of pleasure. They heard someone coming towards the back of the library and they hurried to compose themselves. Elisa grabbed Brian by his arm and they both headed out of the library. Their hearts were racing but the excitement of it all had made Elisa that much more in love with Brian. So much in love that she failed to do her homework. She did not put the two and two's together. Everyone around her was telling her to do the math. Instead she fought against them. Telling them that they were jealous and wished that they had what she and Brian had. She had even fought against her mother who eventually gave in because she did not want the situation to put a wedge between them. But her mother had been right and she deserved to tell

BUMPER TO BUMPER

The day was hot and humid and the last thing that I needed was to be sitting in heavy traffic. I was mad as hell that Rico had missed his bus again for the third time that week. It was not my fault that he had wrecked his car in a chicken race. He was lucky that he had not lost his life although my instinct was to beat the hell out of him when I had found out. I had been on the go all afternoon showing properties to 7clients and my feet along with my head were hurting. I had anticipated on going straight home and lighting a few candles and turning on some soothing music and taking a long and luxurious bubble bath. But instead of soft soothing music my head was filled with the sounds of honking horns and profanity from those who were much like me impatient drivers. I rolled down my windows because we were at a stand still and I was told that you burn more gas with the air conditioning running. The weather was not as hot as my attitude but it was a bit warmer than normal for the month of September. Just when I was about to put my head back on the headrest I felt it. I was rear-ended. I put my head down on the steering wheel and I shook my head and I asked, "God why me?"

I heard the voice at my window and I looked up. He was about six-two, dark mocha chocolate and smelled good enough for me to want to buy whatever he was wearing. He looked at me and when he opened his mouth to speak his beautiful white teeth caught my attention.

He placed his hand on my shoulder and asked, "Ma'am are you alright?"

Pretty white teeth or not I responded, "Hell no I am not alright. Did you or did you not just run into the back of my vehicle? How can I be alright?"

I reached for the handle and pushed the door open. He jumped backwards to avoid being hit in his private area. He gave me a look of concern and I just waved him off with my hand. If I had wanted to hit him with the door I would have. I walked to the rear of my car to assess the damage. Fortunately there had not been any but I had learned from past experiences that you still take their info just in case. He apologized again and we both continued on with our journey. Now I was even angrier with Rico. I was going to blame him for my entire day. Including my aching feet. Finally traffic began to pick up at a steady pace and

I was only ten more minutes from Rico's place of employment. He worked as a teller at one of the banks downtown. I had suggested to him to rent a car but he insisted that it would only be for a couple of days so he would wait and take the bus. He had found a new car but he was having some extra detail work done to it. Well a couple of days had now turned into a couple of weeks because he kept adding or changing things. Today I was going to have to let him know that brother or not, that I was not his personal taxicab. Rico always had a way of taking advantage of me. He was younger than I was but he was not a child anymore. Those little dimples that showed up when he smiled were not going to cut it with me anymore. It was time that I stopped babying him. Rico knew that I loved him and that I would always have his ass but that did not mean that I had to take his shit. I pulled up in front of the bank and waited for him to come out. Ten minutes passed by and he still had not come out. I dialed his cell phone and he did not answer. Just great! First I had to sit in traffic now this. I reached down and felt around for my shoes that I had kicked off of my tired feet. I struggled to get them on and got out of the car and headed into the bank. I said hello to the clerk that was at the entrance and asked if Rico were still there. She pointed to her right and

Rico apologized but I knew that he was still mad and that the ride back to his house was going to be long and quiet. He put his head back onto the headrest and closed his eyes. Yep, it was going to be a long quiet ride. Thirty minutes had gone by and even though I wanted to be tough I did not like the silence. I reached over and nudged Rico and asked him if he wanted to grab a bite to eat. I also added that it would be Dutch. He laughed and agreed to pay his half. We stopped at the Steak Haven Diner. It was only a few blocks away from his apartment building. We walked in and as usual my brother was met with a swarm of, "Hey Rico!" from his female fan club. I just shook my head and Rico with his usual sly grin looked at me and shrugged his shoulders, "What? I can't help it if I got it like that."

I wanted to slap him on the back of his head again but I withheld from doing it. The waitress found us a table and as we walked to the back of the restaurant he stopped and kissed a few of the young ladies on the cheek. Once we were seated I looked at my brother and I was happy for him. Truly happy for him that he had so many friends and acquaintances. It all seemed easy for him but for me I had a difficult time finding and keeping good friends and relationships. I supposed that I was too guarded unlike Rico who lived life for the moment. I would never tell him but sometimes I had wished to be carefree and adventurous like him. He must have caught me starring at him because he waved his hand in front of my face,

"Earth to sister."

I smacked his hand away and we laughed and enjoyed the rest of our time together. I dropped Rico off at his apartment and made a U-turn and headed downtown towards the interstate. Just as I was about to turn at the corner I saw the guy who had hit my bumper. Our eyes caught at the same time. He waved and I nodded. Our eyes did not leave each other's sight until I turned at the corner and my car disappeared under the underpass leading to the interstate. Just as I had pulled into the merging traffic my cell phone rang.

I put my phone on speaker and I said, "Hello."

I had not recognized the number and I definitely did not know the voice but it had a distinct familiarity about it. Inquisitively I asked, "Who is this?"

The voice on the other end identified himself as the young man who had hit my car from behind.

"Oh its' you. The man who made my day."

He chuckled, "Well I would not go as far as to say all of that but I do feel bad about it. I was wondering if you would let me offer to buy you a cup of coffee or perhaps a drink?"

I told him thank you and went on to explain to him that it was not necessary because there had not been any damage done to me or to the car. The more I tried to persuade him that I did not think that there was a need for us to meet he kept trying to make me see things his way.

Finally in his last attempt he offered, "What are the chances of two people meeting twice in one day because one hit the other from behind? And you know what they say?"

I waited for him to tell me but he did not so I played the game and asked, "No what do they say?"

He laughed saying, "I'll tell you over drinks at Sophies' Lounge. Around 8:00 is that okay?"

I hesitated before saying yes. Maybe this would be my opportunity to live Rico's lifestyle just this once. Sophies' Lounge was a quaint little place that a lot of business class people would venture to after a hard day at work. There was usually a jazz band and a mixed crowd of middle aged and older professionals. I had been there once or twice and the food along with its' atmosphere was wonderful. I got off at the next ramp and headed back downtown. I found a parking space in the rear and glanced at my watch. I was early because I would not have had enough time to go all the way home and get back by eight o'clock. I reached into the glove compartment and took out my small make up bag. I freshened up my make up and pumped out a few squirts of my perfume and waited for him to arrive. He pulled up and parked in the only available space that was left on the lot. It was only Thursday and Sophie's was packed. I watched as he got out of his car. His long lean legs stood up and he threw his suit jacket over his shoulder and them proceeded to put it on and adjust its' buttons. He bent over slightly looking into his side mirror and ran his hand across his chin and then through his hair. I watched silently until my elbow hit my horn and he turned around. Oops I thought to myself. He came towards my car and when he reached the door he took the handle and opened it. He reached out his hand to assist me and I thanked him for being a gentleman. We walked around to the front of the restaurant without much being said until we were at the entrance and he opened another door and said, "Pretty ladies first." I was enjoying the chivalry but I also had my radar up. We ordered drinks and decided to share appetizers instead of a full meal. He apologized again for the little accident and once again I let him know that we could move on from it. Maybe that was the catch. Maybe he thought that I was going to sue his insurance company. But after about an hour of eating and chitchatting it turned out that he was just a nice guy. We talked about our jobs, family and why we were both still single. He had a sister much like my brother. He too also wished that he could be carefree but he had his own business and he said that he did not get to be where he was by being frivolous. But I could tell that he had that same yearning as I did. We both just wanted to step outside of our boxes just for one moment to feel the wind in our hair. To do that what was not expected of us. We did have a lot in common and I could see us as being friends. We stayed at Sophie's for about another two to open my thighs. He grabbed a fistful of my hair and tilted my head back and he kissed me. He kissed me without control as if he had been caged. His tongue moving without any rhythm but with an intense hunger. I felt my panties become moisten and I wanted him to remove them immediately and without caution. He could not be safe. Not now because nothing would have been different for us. We were both already use to safe. As if he had read my mind he reached beneath my dress and ripped the delicate lace away from my body. His mouth and tongue had found my breasts that were already plump and waiting. I bit at him and I grabbed his head and pushing him down towards my vagina I ordered him to taste me. He put his arms around my waist and lifted me onto the car. He pushed my dress up and I leaned against my elbows as I watched him devour me. He was rough and I liked it. I liked the way he let his tongue expand and lick my opening and my clit. I wanted to feel every each of him on every inch of my body. The headlights from the passing cars would shine on us periodically and they would honk as they passed by. This turned me on even more. The thrill of letting myself be free was sexually empowering. I was as verbal as he was as his tongue darted in and out of me. I stopped him only when I felt myself coming. He stepped back and

He yelled out of his window, "Hey lady you have something hanging from your bumper."

I gave him a puzzled look and thanked him for the information and drove away.

After a few moments I thought about what the driver had said and then I realized it had to have been my panties. I smiled to myself.

SOMETIMES YOU FEEL
LIKE A NUT

Hayley attached the silver metallic bicycle to the bike rack on the back of her car. She tossed the helmet through the back window onto the rear seat. She proceeded to open the front door on the driver's side but she suddenly remembered that she had forgotten her brothers' wedding gift. She fumbled in her pants pocket to retrieve the keys to her house and realized that she had locked them inside of the house. She kicked the tire of the car and cursed. She was already an hour behind and now this. She was on her way to Ohio to her brothers' rehearsal dinner. Her mother had already scolded her just days before to be prompt. Haley knew that she was not going to hear the end of this. She hurried and ran around to the back of the house and found the flowerpot that held the spare key. She was thankful that her previous housemate had suggested that they hide a spare just in case. She opened the door and went into the living room and there it was still sitting on the end table. She grabbed it and went back through the kitchen making sure the door was locked, she returned the key to the secret place. She stopped dead in her tracks when she remembered that she had still not retrieved the house keys. Well this time they would just have to stay behind because she would miss the entire dinner if she did not get on the road. She ran and jumped into the car and almost took the trashcan and mailbox at the end of the driveway with her. The weatherman had predicted overcast with a thirty-percent chance of rain. She looked up at the sky and it seemed pretty clear. That was a good sign because the last thing she needed was to try and make the two-hour trip on slippery roads. Especially since she knew that she would have to put the pedal to the metal. She pressed the button on the radio and tried to search for the jazz station. The DJ was right on time. He was playing all of her jazz favorites in the next segment. If she had good music and clear traffic she would only be about thirty minutes late give or take a few minutes. She tapped her fingers on the steering wheel and leaned back as she hit the expressway. She could not believe that her big brother was taking the plunge. He was the most confirmed bachelor that she knew. He would preach how he didn't believe in the constitution of marriage. He said he had too much of good lovin' to go around. In fact he said it so often that I named him, "EOE." It stood for equal opportunity egghead. Even though Haley felt that her brother was too big headed way she did. We did everything together that summer. And I did learn to speak Italian and French as a bonus. Not as well as she could of course but she taught me how to roll my tongue so that the words sounded sexy even if I did not pronounce them correctly. I also learned how to french kiss. Apparently I had being doing it incorrectly. Actually I had not done it at all but again Kris was a good teacher. We would be down in the basement alone and we would practice. I was definitely not her first student because she had the skills perfected. One day I was in the shower and the curtain was suddenly pushed back and it was Kris. I stood there with the bar of soap pressed against my breast and my mouth open. Kris stood in front of me bare ass and all. Her skin was flawless. Her black satin hair hung just above her shoulders and her bangs slanted across her eyes. Once I closed my mouth I said, "Oh hey Kris, I'll be out in a minute." She stepped into the shower with me and the next thing I knew her mouth was on mine. We French kissed for what seemed liked forever before I felt her fingers slide against my thigh and then to the opening of my vagina. I had heard about women who liked women but this was something I had never actually experienced. Hell I was still a virgin. Things were happening between my legs that I had read about in wet hair and moved my body pressing it into her face. She licked me and then in one move she inserted her tongue. She moaned as she pushed it in. It felt as if she were trying to reach my navel. With my mouth open I threw my head back and almost choked on the water. I lost my balance but she grabbed my buttocks and she continued licking and sucking me with fury. I grabbed a fistful of her hair, with my jaw locked and wide I screamed, "Oh God, Oh God!" She released me. I wanted to practice some more but Kris showered and left the bathroom. For the rest of the summer we were lovers. When Kris returned to Italy we kept in touch once in awhile until what happened that summer became a blur. I had grown up and had moved away when she returned to Ohio to finish her Masters. She once again stayed in my parents' home and that is where she and Anthony became friends and eventually inseparable lovers. I pulled into the driveway of my parents' home and I could see everyone gathered in the backyard. The smoke hovering over the brick wall told me that my dad had once again burned the steaks. The gate opened and Kristina and Anthony walked out. I looked at the both of them. They were so happy and in love. After the hot steamy summer that Kris and I had I would have sworn that she loved the ladies. She smiled back at me and winked. Um, I wonder? It placed my head upon my pillow I would pray to wake and not to die. Yes I sang for the entire world to hear. Etta and I singing together with all of our heart in unison and I dared to change her words to make the song my own, "At last my love of myself has come along." The night was beautiful and still young and so was I. I was done with the crying and the self-pity. I was tired of blaming myself for not seeing signs that had been there. Some of them should have been more obvious. But there was no longer a point or a need to dwell in a past that I could not change. I had to pick myself up from the deep hole that I had placed myself into. As soon as I realized that he was a big pile of shit I took his ass to the dump and left him there with his stink. It was now the time to mend my heart and move forward. Etta had finished her singing but I still had about two hours to drive before I reached my destination. My stomach as well as my gas tank needed to be filled so I pulled off at the next gas and food exit. I circled around trying to find a gas station that offered the lowest price. I pulled up to the pump and got out of my car and stretched. I walked around to the pump and placed the nozzle into the tank and I leaned against the car. I did not realize how tired I was beginning to feel and I closed my eyes for a minute to rest them. I opened them when I heard the pump click off. I grabbed my receipt and before getting back into my car I glanced around quickly to see what food places were available. I decided to grab some fast food that I could nibble on in the car and headed back onto the interstate. The flow of the traffic was pretty good and I wondered how many of the travelers were heading to the same place that I was. I popped a fry into my mouth and placed another old school jam into the CD player. I moved my shoulders to the music and thoughts form my old college days crept through my mind. Those were the days when I would party all night long from Friday to Sunday. Monday was sleep all day. The rest of the week I was busting my behind in Forensic Science. I missed those days and the many friends that I had made but over the years I had lost contact. We had one class reunion but many of the crew that I had hung out with had not come. Even though they were not there it was still entertaining to see the old photographs that they had lined the banquet halls with. Including my own photo, which was hilarious. My body was as big as a toothpick and my hair was every which way and loose. I had developed and filled out so much more since then. My breasts were not large but they were full as well as my thighs. My hair was now cut short and cropped in a wavy style. I was not what you would call a brick had been given to someone else and because it was Saturday they had to transport another rental vehicle of similarity from across town that took almost two hours. Needless to say I received a substantial discount which meant a little more, "Cha-ching in my pocket for shopping." I pulled up to the circle in front of the building and a nice looking gentleman hurried around to my side of the car to open my door. I swung my shapely legs around and he extended his hand to help me out. I noticed his nicely polished smile and also his obvious eyes as they fell to my legs. I smiled and eased slowly out of the car giving him an opportunity to take it all in. I thought to myself, he hasn't seen anything yet. I thanked him and handed him my keys so that he could remove my bags from the trunk. The valet followed me inside with the baggage cart so that I could check in. The resort lobby was spectacular. It was all enclosed glass with a breathtaking view of the ocean. People were walking along the pathway with fruity drinks and mingling with one another. A few were relaxing in the lobby with books and newspapers while some were waiting to be taken to their rooms. I could only hope that my room would have an identical view. I followed the valet to the elevator and once inside I spoke to him, 'This is absolutely gorgeous."

He turned and looked out of the window as the elevator lifted us up.

He adjusted the baggage cart so that he could get a better view of me before responding, "Yes this is one of the best resorts here. I work here on the weekends and I take courses during the week."

I looked at him and I nosily asked, "Oh, what are you studying?"

He seemed flattered that I was interested and answered back, "I am studying to be a fireman."

It was not until he said fireman that I noticed his muscular build. He smiled and I could see him being a fireman. He was cute. He was not necessarily handsome but more kind of an adorable cute. The elevator doors opened and I followed the back of his body and the baggage cart down the hall to my room. He extended his hand for the key card and opened the door. Handing it back to me, he then stepped aside so that I could walk in. I was so delighted that I actually did a full spin in the middle of the floor. The view was just as I had wished for. The room was decorative and modern, not like the old mom and pop hotel, motel and Inns. This was not just a place you wanted to sleep but a place you wanted to live. I kicked off my shoes and if he had not been standing there I would have been butt—ass naked. I gave him a substantial tip and he vowed to take care of my every need while he was there working for that weekend. After he had left I heard him ask one of the other valets as they passed through the hall, "Damn man did you see that fine honey in suite 212?"

I did not wait to hear the response to the question because I was impatiently headed to the balcony. I opened the French doors and the smell of the salt from the ocean welcomed my senses and my journey to a new life. This called for a drink. I went to the fully stocked bar and selected cognac. I then pulled off my top exposing my red bra and then I unzipped my skirt and let it fall to the floor and adjusted my matching thong. I picked up the skirt and tossed it gently in the direction of the sofa. Picking up my glass of cognac I took a whiff of its' smooth aroma and walking back out onto the balcony I stretched out on the chaise lounger and took all of the night in one star at a time. I woke to the sounds of rolling carts and roaring vacuum cleaners. I heard the twist of the doorknob and I scurried inside to cover myself up. I had apparently fallen asleep out on the balcony. Probably from being tired after the long drive and the shot of cognac that I had. I heard the voice yell out, "Hello, hello!"

From behind the bedroom door I announced that I was still in the room.

The voice yelled out again, "Oh I am so sorry. The do not disturb sign was not placed on your door."

I opened the door a little further and responded to the voice, "Oh no, it's alright. I forgot to put it out last night. Can you return later?"

The door closed and I went to make sure that I put the do not disturb sign in the slot on the door before taking a shower. The morning was everything that I had imagined that it would be and I could not wait to get my feet into the clear blue-green ocean water. I opened my luggage and took out my toiletries and then I dug down to the middle and took out my crochet knitted thong bikini. I was going to turn some heads with this skimpy peek-a-boo attire. I did not think that it would arrive in time for me to bring on the trip but it came just in the nick of time. I went into the bathroom and turned the shower on. The showerhead was huge and the water resembled that of the rain forest. I stepped inside and let the water engulf me. I stood beneath it and I closed my eyes as the water flowed and tickled the nipples of my breast. I raised my head towards the sky and I felt the water as it flounced over and around my forehead and cheeks. I felt the drops tug teasingly at the corners of my mouth trying to get in. I pulled at my nipples that had hardened and begged to be touched. I palmed my supple mounds and pushed them together so that the water made a stream that flowed downward into my valley. I heard myself moan. My fingers slowly and seductively followed my flat stomach like a map, which led my fingers to my valley. I arched my back so that the force of the water pummeled my clit giving off a sensation that beckoned me to open my legs wider and to touch myself. I slid one of my hands between my thighs as the other continued to stroke my breasts and just as I was about to enter myself I felt a hand stop me. I opened my eyes not startled because I could smell his scent of musk. I knew that he was there. Naked dark chocolate silky skin, penis drawn strong and erect ready to please. He placed my hand on his penis and I stroked him as he kissed my mouth full and savagely. Our kisses were as wet and moist as

NINE ONE ONE

Sheila rested her feet on the back of the faded blue cushioned chair. She tried to move her body to a comfortable position but she had just been sitting too long and her back was now aching. She was bored and hungry and the program on the television was in a language that she could not understand. The emergency waiting room was overcrowded and it was hot and musty. No wonder people were sick. You would think that a hospital would have much better circulation she thought to herself. She heard the siren in the distance coming closer and closer and she knew that it would be another two hours wait if this were a life and death situation that they were bringing in. She heard the scuffling of feet and she turned to position herself so that she was now facing the entranceway. The paramedics literally leaped from the ambulance and removed the stretcher from the rear. When they rolled it in she noticed a hand covered with blood as it fell from under the white covers. She shivered because she had always had a sensitive stomach whenever she saw blood. She had not realized how much she had been starring until she felt eyes looking at her. She looked up and caught the glimpse of one of the paramedics. She offered a soft smile but he frowned as if he were disappointed that she could be so nosey. She turned her back to him embarrassed that she had been. Soon things quieted down again and boredom returned. She stood to stretch and yawn and she walked away from her seat and approached a wall that had been smothered with pictures. They were pictures of what seemed to be the hospital employees. It looked as if they had some sort of gathering perhaps a holiday or a convention. There were no visible signs of decorations to indicate a holiday so she concluded it was a convention. She looked at the faces as if she might recognize someone in hopes that if she did, she could complain about how long of a wait it is in the emergency room. Even though she knew that there was no sense in complaining because this was nothing new and surely it was not going to change. Probably not in her lifetime anyway. She walked along the wall and just as she was ready to return to her seat, she heard a voice ask, "See anyone you know?"

She turned and it was the paramedic who had given her the evil eye.

She gave him a smile; "No I was just bored. Nothing else much to do."

He extended his hand in which held a cup of coffee in it. She held up her hand and told him no thanks because she was more of a tea drinker.

He took a sip of the coffee and frowned. He told her, "Um, maybe I should have tasted this before I offered it to you."

Then they both laughed.

She added, "Well at least I am in the right place if I am going to get sick."

He looked around for a trash can to dispose of the cup and stepped away from her momentarily and then he returned. He extended his hand again and introduced himself. His name was Brian and he had just completed his shift. She told him her name and she explained to him her reason for being there. Her neighbor had fallen and thought that she might have a sprained or broken ankle so she had driven her to the emergency room. Just as she and Brian had taken a seat back in the waiting area her neighbor appeared. Her ankle was bandaged but it was not broken. She thanked Brian for his offer of the coffee and for his company. Sheila looped her arm through her neighbors to assist her and Brian immediately grabbed a wheelchair and once again, being a gentleman he offered to push her to the car. Sheila liked that. She was impressed by his clean-cut look and his *'mama raised me right'* charm. He helped her neighbor into the car and closed the door before walking Sheila to the drivers' side.

"Thanks again Brian for being so attentive. I appreciate that in a man," she said as she slid into the seat. Brian placed his hand on the handle of the door and before he closed it he handed her a card with his name and number on it. He smiled at her and then he closed the door with the hopes that she would call him and that it would be much sooner than later.

Sheila brushed the crumbs from her desk as she finished the last bite of her cracker. She was now wishing that she had packed her lunch but she was too tired when she arrived home from the hospital. She had thought about asking one of her co-workers to run out for fast food but she was trying to stick to her New Years resolution and only eat fresh and healthy foods. Plus it was so expensive to always eat out. She reached down and grabbed her purse from under the desk and looked around in it for her wallet. After finding it amongst all of her junk, as she pulled it out and the card that Brian had given her dropped onto her lap. She picked it up and read the information on it. "*Brian Coleman,*" she said his name to herself. She liked that. It had a nice ring to it. She wondered what he was doing. She wondered if he was in the ambulance with the sirens blaring. She decided to give him a call. She dialed the number on the card and his voice mail came on.

"This is Brian. I am sorry that I am unavailable to answer your call but please leave a message. Beep." Nothing fancy about that. That was a good sign. It was plain and to the point. None of that loud rap music or unfunny jokes that is often recorded on people's voicemail. She left a brief message and tucked the card back into her wallet. She decided to skip lunch and take a power nap instead. She adjusted her seat to a recline position and kicked off her shoes. She rubbed her toes together and leaned back closing her eyes. She hoped that she would not have to go to the emergency room ever again.

The phone rang and Sheila leaned forward in the chair. She was a little disoriented. Her power nap had turned into an hour-long sleep. The phone rang again before she realized that it was her cell phone and not the one on her desk. She fumbled under her desk to grab her pocketbook and to find her cell phone that was buried somewhere in all of its contents.

"Girl what are you doing?" I have been buzzing you for the last ten minutes."

Sheila raised up and not clearing her head she bumped it on the corner of the desk. She cursed and looked up at the voice that was leaning and speaking to her over her desk.

"I have been here all day. I didn't even go to lunch."

The girl in the Burberry suit responded, "Uh-huh, another one of those power naps. I don't know why you are always so tired. I could understand if you had a man busting that *thang'* all night."

She made a back and forth movement with her hips as she laughed. Sheila however did not find it funny especially since her head was now throbbing. She rubbed her head and finally finding her cell phone but not before it had stopped ringing, she searched for her missed call. The screen lit up and it displayed the name Brian Coleman. She smiled to herself and then she looked at the lady in the Burberry suit.

"Keisha, why are you in my office?"

Keisha put her hands on her hips, "Because you told me to buzz your office at two o'clock. I buzzed and buzzed but you did not answer. Why you gonna tell somebody to buzz you and you don't answer?"

Sheila cleared her throat and rubbed her head again. "I asked you to buzz me because I need you to take dictation before you leave today. Did you bring your pad?"

Keisha frowned, "No, How was I supposed to know to bring it. You just said to buzz you. I can go back and get it. You are lucky that you are my sister 'cause I wouldn't go all the way back over there for anybody else."

Sheila looked at Keisha as if she were looking at something from out of space. "All the way back? Keisha your office is next door. You are really a piece of work."

Keisha did a slow turn as if she were modeling on a runway and slapped her behind, "I know," she said as she left the room.

Sheila picked up her cell phone and dialed Brian's number again. The voice mail answered again.

"Damn it!" Sheila said. "Hey Brian, this is Sheila again. Sorry that I missed your call. I will try to reach you again later. Bye."

Keisha walked into the room with an inquisitive look on her face and asked, "Who is Brian?"

Sheila giving her the evil eye said, "Nun-ya."

Brian never called back after Sheila had tried again for the third time so she decided to give up. It was now Saturday morning and she decided that she needed to go for a run. She did a few warm-up stretches, grabbed her water bottle and strapped it to her and dropped her keys into her Fannie-pack and headed out of the back door. She put the ipod in her pocket and the headphones in her ears and she ran through the neighborhood at a moderate pace. Once she reached the park she was tired and sweaty. She stopped at a

it wavered through her nostrils. The flames from the candles flickered and their shadows danced upon the walls. She leaned back on the neck pillow and let the sounds of the jazz coming from the radio ease her into a deep relaxation. She drifted off into a dream. A dream of Brian there in the room seductively bathing her. His hands covered in lather slowly moving up her leg as he made his way to her thighs. Rubbing her gently as he squeezed the sponge so that the soapy lather trickled between her opening. She felt the water swish and he playfully splashed it at her opening. She squeezed her legs together as he brushed the texture of the sponge through her fine pubic hair. Teasing her, knowing that she ached for him to be inside of her. He held the sponge above her breast and then he squeezed it once again so that a stream flowed over and in between her two ample mounds tickling her nipples. She raised her knees and twitched her buttocks against the bottom of the tub so she could feel the pressure of the water as it bounced against her vaginal opening. It was warm and cool and then warm and cool again. She needed him to enter her. To come deep inside of her and feel her wetness. To move her body to the rhythm of that of the waves that pummeled against her. She needed him to satisfy that ache which lay deep within her that her own fingers could not reach. She arched her back and the water splashed against the sides of the tub like a tsunami and she cried out as she pressed her thighs tightly around her hands to keep them locked in that space. She shivered and her knees fell to the sides of the tub. The water calmed along with her heartbeat. She drifted off, only this time into a peaceful sleep. Sheila shivered as she stepped out of the tub. The water had turned cold and her fingers and toes were wrinkled like raisins. She grabbed the thick body length towel and wrapped it around her. She walked over to her bed grabbing the lotions and creams from her dresser as she walked past it. She lathered her body with them and then she sprayed herself with one of her many expensive perfumes. She pulled the knotted turban from her hair and pulled her now moisturized curls out and about her face and head. They dangled like miniature springs in colors of light and dark brown. She shook her head to make them swing and then she fluffed through them with her fingers. Walking over to her closet she pushed the clothes that hung neatly on the hangers from left to right then right to left. She was indecisive about what to wear. She did not know whether or not to dress conservative or bold and sexy. She reached to push the clothes once again and her cell phone rang. She sprinted to the bed to retrieve her phone, "Hello?" She smiled. It was Brian.

"Hey beautiful" he started off. "I was just checking in to make sure that you had not changed your mind or anything."

Sheila pulled the phone from her ear and placed it on speaker and returned to the closet. Looking over her shoulder she asked across the room, "And why would I do that?"

Brian chuckled, "I don't know, but it's best to be safe than sorry."

Sheila huffed and let out a sigh. "You might be right because I can't find a thing to wear. How should I dress Brian?"

There was a pause. Sheila walked over to the phone thinking that it had disconnected but it had not. "Brian?" She repeated.

Clearing his voice and shaking the naked image of her from his mind, "Oh I'm sorry. That was one of those loaded questions. I don't know you well enough yet to tell you what I would want you to wear. I will just say that anything you select I know that I will be pleased. I'll see you soon," and he hung up.

Sheila looked down at the phone and pressed the end button. Sheila tapped her lower lip with her finger and thought, so he could not tell me what he really wanted me to wear. Um that means dress extra sexy. And that's exactly what she did.

The lights were dim but they lit the way through the crowd as Sheila walked towards Brian. He stood as she approached him. She could not tell if he was looking at her cleavage that was deepened by the form fitting hip hugging mini dress that she was wearing or if he was captivated by her long and shapely legs that it barely covered up. She could have sworn that she saw drool. Brian met her midway and without any hesitation he let the other men in the room know that she was hands off. He took her arm and folded it into his and led her to their table that was waiting. It was adorned with not one but two dozen of roses. And to top it off he had ordered a bottle of chilled champagne. Impressive to say the least. They chatted through dinner and became familiar with one another. They finished the champagne and with regrets, decided that it was time to end the night. Brian stood and pulled the seat back so that Sheila could stand. He allowed her to lead the way so that he could get a good glimpse of her statuesque figure as she walked away from the table. She knew that he would be watching so she gave him a little extra swing in her movement. He wipe his hand across his forehead, that was now covered with beads of sweat that he knew did not come from drinking too much champagne. He could feel the tightness growing in his pants and he willed his mind somewhere else. He was glad to be out in the cold air because that helped to slow his arousal. He walked Sheila to her car. She noticed an ambulance parked in the lot and she pointed to it and asked, "Is that you?"

Brian looking a bit embarrassed answered back, "Yes but no. I have my own car but I have to go on duty at five a.m. so I was just going to head over to the station from here."

Sheila leaned against the door of her car and there was a moment of awkward silence. Brian moved in closer to her and gave her a quick peck on the lips. When she did not resist he moved his body closer until he was pressed against hers and he kissed her again. First slow and gentle until he felt her urging him to kiss her deeply. He grabbed her hips and as he pushed his tongue deep into her mouth he felt himself harden. He knew that she could feel his thickness and his hands pulled her dress up so that her panties were slightly exposed. He wanted to finger her because he knew that she would be wet. He wanted to finger her and taste her goodness. He wanted to hoist her up onto the car and watch her make faces as he pushed his throbbing muscle in and out of her. Sheila winded and heated pushed him away.

She cleared her throat, "We should say goodnight. I almost forgot where we are. I had a wonderful evening and thank you for the beautiful roses."

Brian reached in to kiss her again but Sheila put her hands between them.

She put her finger to his lips and said, "Good things come to those who wait."

She turned away from him and got into her car and drove away. She looked into her rearview mirror and watched as Brian got into the ambulance. She stopped at the red light and while she was waiting for it to change she called Brian. He glanced at the number on the screen before answering.

"Hello, hello? Sheila?"

Sheila moaned into the phone, "I have a 911 emergency!"

Brian grinned and turned on the red flashing light, "What's your emergency ma'am?"

Sheila smiled and placed her hand between her thighs, "I'm on fire."

TO LOVE ME

Taking the time to love me
why is it such a difficult task?
Showing me affection
should never be too much to ask

Putting your heart into it
should be a pleasure not an endless chore
my need for your undivided attention
never should be ignored

Caresses should be automatic
yet we seem to have to plan them in advance
our affection should be spontaneous
new ideas you're afraid to chance

Lets be passionate with our love
and throw caution to the wind
we are both consenting adults
there is no need for us to pretend

So embrace me with your passion
be fearless with your fantasies
welcome me into your open arms
and take the time to love me.

NEVER SATISFIED

Lacie held onto the metal headboard as her husband bounced her around as she sat on top of him. She tried to shut his words out of her mind as he told her of his fantasy of watching her being pleasured by someone other than himself. Although this was a turn on for him she was annoyed. She had heard it so many times before that it was like a broken record. There was never anything new. It was as if she was watching the same movie over again. The script was always the same. She already knew the ending. She wanted to scream at him and to tell him to shut the hell up. Instead she just wished for the entire experience to be over. Just once she wanted their lovemaking to be passionate. She wanted to feel the magic that she carried around in her head. She knew that he thought that he was the *'Man'* and that he was good at doing his thing. But that was what the issue was. It was just a thing that they did. The emotional connection was missing. He always wanted to bring someone else into their bed. It was not that she did not want to indulge in his fantasy but she needed to be satisfied solely and soulfully by him before she could share their intimacy with anyone else whether it was real or fantasy. She

360

had tried to let him know in so many subtle ways but they just went beyond him. Her husband in all of the thirty years that they had been married had never satisfied her. He could bring her to orgasm orally but she wanted to experience a vaginal orgasm with him deep inside of her. She wanted to feel him grab onto her and hold tightly as she pressed her wet vagina around his throbbing penis. She did not understand how he could not know that she could not share in any other fantasy because her fantasy was of him. The fantasy that he would grab onto her small breasts and lick her nipples and then take them fully into his mouth and bite them, causing her only enough pain to bring her pleasure. That she needed him to grab her hair and pull her head back as he placed intimate kisses along her neck. She wanted to feel his nails rake down her back until they reach her round buttocks. She wanted him to slap them and let her know that they were his as he grabbed a fistful of her flesh into his hands. She was so deeply in love with him that she could not think of anyone else to bring her that kind of pleasure. Finally the bed stopped shaking and her husband let out a sigh as if he had just put in a hard day at work. She rolled over onto the bed beside him and as she stared up at the ceiling a tear rolled down the side of her face. He let out another sigh as if he had just had the best sex ever and she wondered if he was pretending. He had told her once before that she was frigid. Lacie used the corner of the sheet to wipe away the tear that had now multiplied into tears. She wanted to tell him that she was not frigid but that she was instead fucking frustrated. But what could she say. She had gone too many years with letting him believe that he was *'The Man'* when it came to their lovemaking. She felt him turn away from her and then she heard the familiar sound of his snoring. He never spooned her or held her in his arms after they had made love. Perhaps that was because it was not truly lovemaking. She felt that her sex life with him was like a shoe commercial—Just Do It. She lay there listening to his snoring and she touched herself until she brought herself to the orgasm that he had left lingering between her thighs. Morning had come and Lacie heard the sounds of her husband moving around in the shower. She lifted the covers over her head to shield out the light and the previous night's disappointment. She had just begun to drift back to sleep when she felt her husbands' lips touch hers lightly. She opened her eyes and threw her arms about his neck and she squeezed him not wanting to let him go. Oh God how she loved this man. She released him and watched him as he left from her sight. She heard the front door close and she leaped out of the bed and ran to the window. She watched him get into the car and then drive away. She wanted to call him back. She wanted him to run up the stairs and pick her up and toss her back onto the bed where he would devour her. Spreading her legs open he would climb on top of her and he would whisper into her ear how much he loved her. She imagined it all in her mind as she felt his hard penis easing into her moist vagina. She felt his hot breath along her earlobe as he told her of all of the nasty and naughty things that he wanted to do to her because she was his fantasy. She wished hard and long but after moments of waiting she knew that he would not return. She fell back against the bed and feeling defeated she cried yet again. Morning had become the afternoon and Lacie pulled herself from under the covers and headed into the bathroom. She looked at herself in the mirror and she knew that she was tired of being frustrated. She was tired of never being satisfied. She had loved this man. She had given him her all and she was receiving nothing back. He had to know. Perhaps he was just being selfish. After all he had told her that he thought that she was frigid. Yet he never would elaborate on what he felt she was lacking or even more important what he needed more of from her so that he could on his as he tugged and pulled on the nipples of her breasts as she helped him push her mounds of flesh together. And then when she begged for more he would insert only the tip of his penis as he found the spot that would ignite the fire that would lead them both to the orgasm that she so desired. He would push himself deeper into her and she would feel his thickness as he slid against her wet vaginal walls. Squeezing the muscles between her thighs she would bring him pleasure because she not only wanted him to be loved but to also be satisfied. But this was only a dream for Lacie. A dream that she had longed to come true. Lacie had shared only lies with her girlfriends. They would sit around and talk about how they were all being satisfied by their lovers. She envied them. Lacie would never let them know that she had never experienced the orgasms that they spoke about. She listened as they told of their encounters in the back seat of their cars, or pulling over onto the side of the road and being entered from behind as their bodies were sprawled across the hood. They made it all sound so easy and natural when they spoke about their quickies in public places. Some of their encounters would bring moisture between her legs as she imagined exchanging places with them. They spoke of how they would have multiple orgasms as their breast she aged she wondered if she ever would. She stood at the patio doors and watched as the pool guy dragged the long vacuum hose across the floor of the swimming pool. His tan body from the waist up was exposed and the sun glimmered on the beads of sweat that drizzled down his back. Lacie watched his movements as he pushed the vacuum backwards and forwards in a slow motion. She daydreamed about her husband moving inside of her with that same movement. The pool guy turned and caught a glimpse of her watching and he nodded. Lacie nodded back and smiled. Their eyes locked for a moment that Lacie thought was a little too long and she closed the blinds. Her panties were moist and for a flitting moment she wondered what it would be like to walk through those doors and drop her robe. She leaned her head against the glass pane and in her mind she felt his breath as he moved his fingers along her neck. She felt the chill of his tongue as he licked at her breast. She suddenly felt guilty and ashamed that she could have those thoughts and she shook her head no and she ended her daydream. Many men offering her good sex had often approached her. Many of them had been her husbands' colleagues. It was as if they knew that her husband was not meeting her needs. None the less she had never considered or entertained the idea of being craved for so much more. This was the moment where he would lift her off of her feet and lead her to the stairs and undress her along the way. He would not wait until they were in the privacy of their bedroom or on the comfort of satin sheets. She imagined feeling the roughness of the carpet as it rubbed against her skin as he pushed her back onto the stairs. Her heart beat as she waited with hope and anticipation that he would pull her legs up and around his shoulders and would make savage love to her. He would look into her eyes and see her needs and not just his own. But he did not move. Lacie lingered in his embrace giving him a few more moments. She pressed her body next to his rubbing him seductively hoping to feel his penis rise and thicken. In her mind the words were pleading and she hope that he could read them loud and clear. Take me. Take me with a vengeance. Yet once again she would be disappointed. She needed him to be spontaneous and aggressive. She needed him to do what other men had whispered to her of what they wanted and would do if given the opportunity.

Instead he did nothing except kiss her gently on her forehead and asked, "What's for dinner? I hope that it is good whatever it is because I am starved."

She was starved too but his stallion never left the gate. She gently eased out of his arms and restraining her tears she looked up at her husband who had no clue what so ever of her yearning and she smiled. As she walked away knowing that she loved him and had always been loved by him she also knew that she would never be satisfied the way that she needed to be by him. She turned and walked towards the patio door and re-opened the blinds. She stood with her forehead pressed against the glass pane and she wondered when the pool guy would return again.

What will Lacie do? Will she remain faithful and unsatisfied or will she take a dip into the pool? What would you do?

Stiletto Nights Too
The Fire Below

Coming soon

ABOUT THE AUTHOR

Shyy is a creative author who enjoys writing short stories. Each one is like a morsel of chocolate. Just enough to satisfy one's craving but leaving them wanting more. Her unique style of writing will keep you intrigued.